"You don't think I feel anything, Isabella?" Adham's voice was soft, as tightly reined in as the rest of him.

He drew his finger over the line of her jaw, his dark eyes intent on hers, and then she felt the first crack in his facade. A slight tremor in his hand unveiled fear in his eyes.

"I feel things I have no business feeling. I want things that are not mine to covet."

MAISEY YATES knew she wanted to be a writer even before she knew what it was she wanted to write.

At her very first job she was fortunate enough to meet her very own tall, dark and handsome hero, who happened to be her boss, and promptly married him and started a family. It wasn't until she was pregnant with her second child that she found her very first Harlequin Presents® book in a local thrift store—by the time she'd reached the happily ever after, she had fallen in love. She devoured as many as she could get her hands on after that, and she knew that these were the books she wanted to write!

She started submitting, and nearly two years later, while pregnant with her third child, she received The Call from her editor. At the age of twenty-three she sold her first manuscript to Harlequin Presents, and she was very glad that the good news didn't send her into labor!

She still can't quite believe she's blessed enough to see her name on not just any book, but her favorite books.

Maisey lives with her supportive, handsome, wonderful, diaper-changing husband and three small children across the street from her parents and the home she grew up in, in the wilds of southern Oregon. She enjoys the contrast of living in a place where you might wake up to find a bear on your back porch, then into the home office to write stories that take place in exotic, urban locales.

THE INHERITED BRIDE

MAISEY YATES

~ KINGS OF THE DESERT ~

Harlequin®

TORONTO NEW YORK LONDON
AMSTERDAM PARIS SYDNEY HAMBURG
STOCKHOLM ATHENS TOKYO MILAN MADRID
PRAGUE WARSAW BUDAPEST AUCKLAND

If you purchased this book without a cover you should be aware
that this book is stolen property. It was reported as "unsold and
destroyed" to the publisher, and neither the author nor the
publisher has received any payment for this "stripped book."

Recycling programs
for this product may
not exist in your area.

ISBN-13: 978-0-373-52814-1

THE INHERITED BRIDE

First North American Publication 2011

Copyright © 2011 by Maisey Yates

All rights reserved. Except for use in any review, the reproduction or
utilization of this work in whole or in part in any form by any electronic,
mechanical or other means, now known or hereafter invented, including
xerography, photocopying and recording, or in any information storage
or retrieval system, is forbidden without the written permission of the
publisher, Harlequin Enterprises Limited, 225 Duncan Mill Road,
Don Mills, Ontario, Canada M3B 3K9.

This is a work of fiction. Names, characters, places and incidents are
either the product of the author's imagination or are used fictitiously,
and any resemblance to actual persons, living or dead, business
establishments, events or locales is entirely coincidental.

This edition published by arrangement with Harlequin Books S.A.

For questions and comments about the quality of this book
please contact us at Customer_eCare@Harlequin.ca.

® and TM are trademarks of the publisher. Trademarks indicated with
® are registered in the United States Patent and Trademark Office, the
Canadian Trade Marks Office and in other countries.

www.eHarlequin.com

Printed in U.S.A.

THE INHERITED
BRIDE

Mom, Dad, this one is for you.
Thank you for always believing in me.
If everyone had parents like you,
the world would be a better place.

CHAPTER ONE

HE WASN'T Room Service. That was for sure. Princess Isabella Rossi looked up, way up, at the tall, forbidding man who was standing in the doorway of her hotel room. His muscular frame was displayed to perfection by the tailored black suit he was wearing. But the suit was where any semblance of civilization ended.

His expression was inscrutable, his dark eyes blank, his lips flattened into a firm line. His squared jaw was clenched tight, the tension mirrored in his stance. His golden skin was marred with scars in some places; his cheek, the exposed part of his wrists.

She swallowed hard. "Unless you have my dinner stashed on a cart somewhere, I'm afraid I can't allow you to come in."

He uncrossed his arms and held his hands out, as if to show that they were empty. "Sorry."

"I was waiting for Room Service."

He tapped the top of the door with his open palm. "They make peepholes in these doors for a reason. It's always wise to check."

"Thank you. I'll remember that." She made a move to close the door, but it didn't budge. He was propping it open with his shoulder. She tried to close it again, this time putting more weight behind it. The door still didn't move, and neither did he. His expression did not betray even a hint of strain.

"You've caused a lot of big problems for quite a few people. Including your security detail, who now find themselves without jobs."

Her heart sank into her stomach. He knew who she was. She didn't know whether to be relieved or even more upset by that. Relieved he wasn't here to hurt her, but... but he was here to take her back. Either to Umarah or to Turan, and she didn't want to go to either country. Not now. Not when she'd fallen so short of everything she'd wanted to accomplish.

One night of freedom. That was all she'd gotten. A glimpse of the world as she would never know it.

"Do you work for my father?"

"No."

"You work for Hassan, then." That should have been obvious. Judging by the faint accent that tinged his deep voice, she should have guessed that Arabic was his native language. She should have known that he was in league with her fiancé.

"You're in breach of contract, *amira*. You should have known the Sheikh could not allow such a thing."

"I didn't imagine he would be thrilled about it, but..."

"You did a very foolish thing, Isabella. Your parents were concerned that you'd been kidnapped."

The guilt she'd been holding at bay for the past twenty-four hours made her stomach feel tight. But with that tightening came a strange fluttering sensation that seemed to grow stronger when she looked into those dark, fathomless eyes. She looked down. "I didn't mean to scare anyone."

"And what did you think would happen when you

disappeared? That everyone would go about their daily lives as if nothing had happened? You did not believe that your own parents would be frantic with worry?"

She shook her head mutely. In truth, she'd known her family would be upset, but she hadn't considered that they'd *worry* about her. Be angry, yes. She'd imagined they would be angry. That they might be afraid the sheikh would want to renege on their bargain if there was a chance she'd been out in the big bad world long enough to become *damaged goods*, or something.

"I...no. I didn't really think they would be worried."

He shifted his focus to the hallway, to a young couple standing a few doors down, kissing passionately against the wall. "I am not going to continue this discussion in the hallway."

She sneaked a glance at the passionate duo and her face began to burn with embarrassment. "Well, I can't let you in!"

He looked past her and into the simple room. "Slumming it?"

"No. This is a perfectly nice hotel. Anywhere too up-market and—"

"They would have known who you were. And they would have wondered."

She nodded mutely.

"I will be coming in," he continued. "With your permission or without it. One thing you'll learn about me very quickly, Princess. I don't take orders."

"There are two months and ten days until the wedding," she said, desperation clawing at her. "I need...I need this time."

"You should have considered that before you ran away."

"I didn't *run away*. That makes me sound like a naughty child."

"Then what would you call it?" He looked down the long corridor, back at the couple, whose activities had heated up in the past minute, and then back at her. "I'm waiting to be let in. I find I've been extremely patient."

She could tell from the fierce glint in his eyes that he absolutely would push his way into the room if she didn't allow him access. She could tell by all of the barely harnessed power of the body, the strength that was radiating from him, that he was only seconds away from doing it.

A sound that could only be described as ecstatic came from the couple in the hall, and Isabella jumped slightly, releasing her hold on the door.

"Wise decision." He stepped past her and into the small hotel room.

He stood rigid, his posture straight, his expression neutral. He was handsome. Extremely handsome. She realized that now. She'd been so struck by the immensity of his power, the energy that seemed just to radiate from him, that she hadn't had the time to really look at him. But she was looking now.

Now that his mouth was relaxed she noticed that his lips were full and well shaped, even with the small scar running through a corner of his mouth. He had the darkest eyes she'd ever seen. Nearly black, and so intensely focused that she felt as though he could see everything about her—as if he was looking into her. He was the sort of man who evoked a visceral reaction that was impossible to fight or ignore; one she didn't fully understand, and one she definitely didn't know what to do with.

"I wasn't letting you in. I was startled, that's all." she

said, hoping she sounded at least mildly imperious. She was a princess; she ought to be able to do imperious.

"I did tell you I was coming in regardless of whether you wanted me to or not."

She cleared her throat and focused on a spot just past him. Everything seemed to slow down a bit as she looked at him. Even the air felt thicker, making breathing a labored thing. He was just so… He was a force rather than a person. "Yes, well, now you're in."

"Yes. I am. And we're leaving."

She took one step backward. "I'm not going with you."

One black eyebrow shot up. "You think not?"

"Are you going to carry me out of here?"

He shrugged. "If I have to."

The thought of being touched, held closely by this man, this stranger, was entirely off-putting.

She took another step backward, trying to put some space between them. "I don't really think you would do that."

"Make no mistake, Princess, I would. You have a binding agreement with the High Sheikh of Umarah, and I have been charged with bringing you to him. That means you're coming with me one way or another. Even if I have to carry you kicking and screaming down the streets of Paris."

She stiffened, trying to look composed, trying to hide the nerves that were making her hands shake. "I don't think you would do that either."

He leveled that intense focus onto her. "Keep issuing challenges and we'll see just what I will and won't do."

He appraised her slowly, his gaze lingering on her curves. Something about the way he looked at her, the way his eyes glittered in the dim light, made her feel like she was exposed, like she was undressed.

Her heart rate sped up, something unfamiliar and hot racing through her bloodstream, making her pulse soar. Her heart was pounding so loud she was almost certain that he must hear it. She sucked in a deep breath, trying to calm herself, trying to slow her racing blood.

She looked away from him, trying to grab a shred of sanity that might be lying around somewhere in the corner of her mind. And her eyes locked onto the big bed that was in the corner of the room. It made her think of the lovers out in the hall. Blood roared into her face, and she could feel her heart beating in her temples, her cheeks so hot they burned.

Focus!

She had to get her thoughts together, had to figure out a way to get rid of this man and get back to the business of living her life before she had to sacrifice it all in the name of duty. The heavy diamond on her finger, delivered by courier six months ago, was a constant reminder of the fact that there was a timer ticking against her freedom. And this man was completely destroying her only hope of actually living for herself.

For two short months she wanted a life that was her own. It was a simple thing, and yet everyone seemed hell-bent on making sure it didn't happen. When she'd actually asked her father if she could have some time his disdain for her request, his immediate refusal—as though it didn't even bear considering—had been horrible. So she had set out to make it happen on her own. She couldn't go with him. Not now. Not when she was so close.

There had to be a way to get him on her side…a way to turn the tide in her favor. But she didn't know anything about men. Not really. The most exposure she'd had to a man had come in the form of her older brother, Max. She *had* seen how her sister-in-law interacted with him, though—how she managed to appeal to Max's softer side when no one else could.

Although, she had her doubts that this man *had* a softer side. But she had to do something.

Taking a breath, she stepped forward and put her hand lightly on his arm. His eyes clashed with hers and a bolt of sensation shot to her stomach. She pulled back quickly, the heat from his skin lingering on her fingertips.

"I'm not ready to go back yet. I have two months until the wedding, and I really want to take this time to...to myself."

Adham al bin Sudar fought down the flash of anger that rose in him. The little vixen was trying to tempt him, to use seduction to get her way. The soft touch against his sleeve hadn't been an innocent action, but a calculated maneuver. One designed to stir a man's blood, make it pump hotter, faster. And when the woman doing the touching looked like Isabella Rossi, how could it not?

He thought, not for the first time, that his brother was an extremely lucky man to have her as his future bride. Although Adham would have been happy enough to take her as a temporary mistress, rather than a wife.

The woman was beautiful, with full, tempting curves and a face that was flawlessly lovely. Her beauty was not subjective, but universal. Her high, classic cheekbones, small upturned nose, and perfectly formed lips were designed to turn heads wherever she went. Even with a total absence of make-up her beauty was enough to rival that of any of the world's great beauties.

She didn't have the fashionable, streamlined look of a supermodel, but he had always preferred his women to look like women. And Isabella Rossi certainly had the shape of a woman. He allowed his eyes to linger on that shape for a while, to appreciate the full, rounded curve of her breasts. Breasts that would lead even the most disciplined of men into sin.

Immediate disgust filled him as he realized what he was doing, blocking out the flood of desire that was making his body harden and his heart race. She was his brother's fiancée. Forbidden in every way. Even looking was not permitted.

Adham's brother had asked him to bring her back for the wedding—had begged him to bring him his future bride so that his honor would not be compromised. That was what he was here to do—though he was beginning to doubt her suitability. A selfish, spoiled child with no sense of duty would not make an appropriate sheikha for his country. But Isabella Rossi came with the allegiance of an entire country—a trade and military alliance that would not come from any other bride. That made her essential, irreplaceable.

"Going off on your own was extremely foolish," he bit out, calling on all his willpower to squash the desire that had risen up in him. "Anything could have happened to you."

"I was safe," she said. "I'll continue to be safe. I'll—"

"You will do nothing but come with me, *amira*. Do you honestly think I would leave you to yourself just because you put on a pretty smile and ask nicely?"

Her lush lips parted in shock. "I...I had hoped that—"

"That you would not be held to your word? If the people of Umarah were to find out that their sheikh's bride has deserted him his honor would be compromised. He would be shamed in the eyes of his people. You might be deemed an unsuitable choice. And if that were to happen, what would become of the alliance? Jobs, money, security, all meant to benefit our people, gone."

She bit down hard on her lower lip, her blue eyes glistening. Annoyance surged through him—a welcome replacement for the sudden physical attraction that had hit him the first moment he'd seen her. He didn't have the patience to deal with emotional women. Emotion in general was useless to him. Although he had a feeling Isabella was employing it as a manipulation technique.

She would soon learn that he was the wrong man to try to soften with tears. Tears meant nothing to him.

"I wasn't going to run out on the wedding. I just wanted some time."

He noticed the way she turned the large solitaire diamond ring around on her slender finger as she spoke. She was still wearing the ring Hassan had sent her—a possible sign that she was telling the truth.

"Time's up, I'm afraid."

The devastation in her eyes would have affected most people. He felt nothing. Nothing but contempt. He'd seen far too much of the world to be swayed by the tears of a poor little rich girl, bemoaning her marriage to an extremely wealthy royal.

"I didn't get to see the Eiffel Tower," she said quietly.

"What?"

"I didn't get to see the Eiffel Tower. I took the train from Italy, and I just arrived here this evening. I wasn't going to go out by myself at night. I didn't see anything of Paris that I wanted to."

"You've never seen the Eiffel Tower?"

She blushed, her sun-kissed cheeks turning a deep rose. "I've *seen* it. But seeing it from a moving motorcade and actually going to it, getting out and experiencing it, are two very different things."

"This isn't a holiday, and I'm not here to give you a guided tour. I'm taking you back to Umarah as soon as possible."

"Please—just let me go to the Eiffel Tower."

It was a simple request. One that could be easily accommodated. And, while he wasn't moved by her drama, he wasn't cruel. It would also make it much easier to remove her from the hotel if she came of her own free will. He wouldn't hesitate to remove her by force, but it was not his preference.

"In the morning. I give you my word I will let you stop there on the way to the airport. But you have to come with me now, and not kicking and screaming."

"And you'll keep your word?"

"Another thing you will learn about me, Princess: I'm not a nice man, and I'm not particularly good company, but I do keep my word. Always. It is a matter of honor."

"And honor is important to you?"

"It's the one thing no one can take from you."

"I'll take that as a yes," she said. He inclined his head in agreement. "And if I don't go with you...?"

"You're going with me. Kicking and screaming optional—as is sightseeing."

"Then I suppose that means my choices are limited." She chewed her bottom lip.

"That's understating it; your choice is singular. The method, however, is up to you."

She blinked furiously, her shoulders sagging in defeat, her eyes averted as if she didn't want him seeing the depth of her pain. Although he was certain that in truth she wanted nothing more than for him to witness just how distressed she was.

"My bags will have to be packed. I've just gotten all of my things put away." She didn't make a move toward the closet, she simply stood rooted to the spot, looking very sad and very young.

"I'm not doing it *for* you," he said sardonically.

Her eyes widened and her cheeks flushed a delicate rose. "I'm sorry. You work for Sheikh Hassan, and I assumed…"

"That I was a servant?"

She mumbled something he thought might have been a curse in Italian, and stalked over to the closet, sliding the lightweight white doors open.

"I don't know how you meant to survive in the real world when you still expect someone else to deal with your clothes for you, Princess."

Her shoulders stiffened, her back going rigid. "Don't call me that anymore," she said without turning.

"It's what you are, Isabella. It's *who* you are."

A hollow laugh escaped her lips. "Who knows who I am? I don't."

He let the comment pass. It wasn't his job to stand around and psychoanalyze his brother's future wife. His duty was to return her unharmed, untouched, and he intended to do that as soon as possible.

He had other matters to attend to. He had geochemists actively searching for the best place to install a new rig, looking for more oil out in the middle of the Umarahn desert. He liked to be there on site when they were making final decisions about location. He didn't micromanage his team, he hired the best. But during major events he liked to be on hand in case there was a problem.

Facilitating the growing Umarahn economy was only half of his job. Protecting his brother, and their people, was his utmost concern. He would give his life for his brother without hesitation. So when Hassan had informed him that his bride had gone missing Adham had offered to ensure she was found. He was now regretting that offer.

She whipped around to face him, a pile of clothing, still on hangers, draped over her arms. "You could help me."

He shook his head slightly, watching as she began to awkwardly fold the clothing and place it in her bag. By the third or fourth article she seemed to develop some sort of method, even if it was unconventional.

"Who packed for you in the first place?"

She shrugged, the color in her cheeks deepening. "One of my brother's servants. I was supposed to leave his home this morning. I just left a few hours earlier."

"And went to an undisclosed location?"

She narrowed her eyes, her lips pursed in a haughty expression. "What did you say your name was?"

"According to the report I read on you, you're a very smart woman. Perfect marks in school. I think you know perfectly well that I didn't offer you my name."

Her delicate brow creased. "I think that, considering you know everything about me from my marks in school and I shudder to think what else, I should at least know your name."

"Adham." He left out his surname, and in so doing his relationship to Hassan.

"Nice to meet you," she said, folding a silk blouse and sticking it in the bottom of a pink suitcase. She paused mid-motion. "Actually, it isn't, really. I don't know why I said that. Habit. Good manners." She sighed. "Because it's what I was *trained* to do." She said it despairingly, her luscious mouth pulled down at the corners.

"You resent it?"

"Yes," she said slowly, firmly. "Yes, I do." She took a breath. "It's *not* nice to meet you, Adham. I wish you would go away."

"We don't always get what we wish for."

"And some of us never do."

"You'll have the Eiffel Tower. That has to be enough."

CHAPTER TWO

ADHAM's penthouse apartment in Paris's seventh district wasn't at all what she'd expected from a man who worked for the High Sheikh. It was patently obvious that he had money of his own, and likely the status to go with it. He was probably a titled man—another sheikh or something. No wonder he'd looked at her as if she was crazy when she'd expected him to collect her things.

That had been mortifying. She hadn't meant to be rude. It was just that she was used to being served. She'd always devoted the majority of her time to studying, reading, cultivating the kinds of skills her parents deemed necessary for a young woman of fine breeding. None of those skills had included folding her own clothes. Or, in fact, any sort of household labor.

She'd always considered herself an intelligent person; her tutors and her grades had always reinforced that belief. But the realization of what a huge deficit she had in her knowledge made her feel…it made her feel she didn't know anything worth knowing. Who cared if you knew the maximum depth of the Thames if you didn't know how to fold your own clothes?

The penthouse didn't provide her with any more clues about the man who was essentially her captor. Unless he really was as sparse and uncompromising as the surrounding décor. Cold as brushed steel, hard as granite. Arid, like the desert of his homeland. That seemed possible.

She looked around the room, searching for any kind of personal markers. There were no family photographs. The art on the walls was modern, generic—like something you might find in a hotel room. There was no touch of personality, no indication as to who he might be, what he liked. That just reinforced her first theory.

"Are you hungry?" he asked, without turning his focus to her.

"Can I get something besides bread and water?"

"Is that what you think, Isabella? That you're my captive?"

She swallowed hard, trying to move the knot that had formed in her throat. "Aren't I?"

Wasn't she everyone's captive? A puppet created by her parents and trained to respond to whoever was pulling the strings.

"It depends on how you look at it. If you try to walk out the door I can't let you. But if you don't make another escape attempt we can exist together nicely."

"I believe that makes me a prisoner."

Her words made no difference to him. It was as though he took a hostage every day of the week. The only change in his facial expression was the compression of his mouth. The scar that ran through his top lip lightened slightly at the pull of his skin, the small flaw in his handsome face only reinforcing the warrior image her mind had created for him.

"Prisoner or not, I was wondering if you might like some dinner. I believe I took you from the hotel before you had a chance to have yours."

Her stomach rumbled, reminding her that she'd been

hungry for a couple of hours now. "I *would* like some dinner."

"There is a restaurant nearby. I have them deliver food whenever I'm here. I assume that will be all right for you?"

"I…" *Now's the time to do it…get what you want now or you'll never have the chance.* "Actually, I'd like to have a hamburger."

His eyebrows lifted. "A hamburger."

She nodded curtly. "Yes. I've never had one. And I'd also like chips. Fries. Whatever you call them. And a soft drink."

"Seems a simple request for a last meal. I think I can accommodate my captive." She thought she might have heard a hint of humor in his voice, but it seemed unlikely. He pulled out his cell phone and dialed, then spoke to whoever was on the other end in polished French.

"You speak French?"

He shrugged. "I keep a residence here. It's practical."

"Do you speak Italian?" she asked, moving to a sleek black sofa that looked about as soft as marble and sitting gingerly on the edge.

"Only a little. I'm fluent in Arabic, French, English and Mandarin."

"Mandarin?"

His lips curved slightly in what she assumed might be an attempt at a smile as he settled in the chair across from her. "That's a long story."

"I speak Italian, and Latin as well, French, Arabic— obviously English."

"You're quite well-educated."

"I've had a lot of time to devote to it." Books had been her constant companion, either at the family home, or for those brief years she'd gone to an all-girl school in Switzerland. Her imagination had been her respite from the demands that her parents had placed on her. From their constant micro-managing of her actions. In her mind at least she'd been free.

But it hadn't been enough lately. She'd needed more. An escape. A reality apart from the life she'd led behind the palace walls. Especially if she was expected to go and live behind more walls, to be shut away again. Set apart. Isolated even when surrounded by hundreds of people.

She shivered, cold loneliness filling her chest, her lungs, making her feel as if she was drowning.

"It's nice to know all those languages when you move in the type of circles my family do. I've gotten to practice them with various diplomats and world leaders." During their frequent trips to Italy they'd always met with politicians, wealthy socialites. The same kind of person, the same sort of conversation. Always supervised. She clenched her fists. "So, what have you used your linguistic skills for?"

Probably for seducing women all over the world...

"They have been a matter of survival for me. In my line of work, understanding the words of the enemy can be a matter of life and death."

A chill settled over her, goosebumps rising on her arms. "You...that's happened to you?"

He gave her a hard look, one void of expression, but conveying an intense amount of annoyance over having to carry on this extended conversation with her. "Yes. I am in the service of my country. My king. It's my job to protect him, and now to protect you."

The fierce loyalty in Adham's voice shocked her. She didn't know if there was anything in the world she felt so much passion for. She'd lived her life by the rules until recently, but she hadn't followed the rules out of any great love for them. She had just done it. Existed. Her future, her marriage, was a given—her duty to her people. But there was no fire of conviction there.

"Is that why you're here? To protect me?"

"He trusts you with me. He would not send just any man to search for his fiancée. He was concerned for your safety. And I will protect you. I will bring you back to him."

"Why is it that everyone seems to think I can't walk from room to room without someone holding my hand?" Frustration pulled at her, making her feel she might explode.

His jaw tightened. "Because you present yourself in such a way that suggests it."

"That isn't fair. I've never been given a chance to make my own decisions. It's assumed I'm incapable."

"If you show as much maturity in the rest of your life as you have with your decision to run from your duty, I can see why."

"I'm not running from my duty. I understand what's expected of me. I even understand why. But I realized something a few weeks ago. I've never been alone. *Ever.* Not really. I've always had a security detail following my every move, chaperones making sure I never put a toe out of line, dressers telling me what to wear, teachers telling me what to think—all leading up to a future that was predestined for me and that I have no control over." Her throat tightened. "I just wanted time. Time to find out who I am."

A buzzing sound echoed in the room, signaling the arrival of their food. Adham stood and walked to the door, punching in a security code that she assumed allowed the delivery man access. In a few moments Adham returned, holding two bags that looked as if they were packed full of food.

She tried to find some of the optimism she'd felt earlier, when she'd first boarded the train from Italy. She only had this one night of freedom, and a very limited amount tomorrow. There would be a lot of time for her to cry later. And she would. For now she was seizing the moment. She was going to enjoy her dinner. A dinner *she* had chosen—not the palace dietician.

Adham set the bags on a glass coffee table and opened them. The smell that filled the room made Isabella's stomach growl more insistently. She lost focus on that, though, as she watched Adham remove the tightly wrapped food from the bag, her eyes transfixed on his hands. They were so masculine, so different from her own. Wide and square, with deep scars marring the golden skin of his knuckles.

What kind of man was he? What had he done to earn so many marks of pain on his body? He'd said he'd been in life-or-death situations. It was clear that he was still alive. Not so clear what had happened to his opponents. Not for the first time she wondered if she should be afraid of him. But she wasn't. He unsettled her. Made her feel a strange sort of jumpiness, as though she'd had one too many shots of espresso—one of the only vices her parents allowed her.

One thing she knew for certain was that she wanted to be rid of the man. No one had babysat her brother while he'd gone out and had his taste of freedom. No one had doubted he would return to do his duty. She would do what she was meant to do. She'd always known that a love match wasn't in her future, even before Hassan had been chosen for her. But that didn't mean she wanted to be kept under lock and key her entire life. A few short weeks was all she'd asked for. A small concession when a lifetime of what amounted to servitude was in her future.

She wasn't going to think about it now. All she was going to do was enjoy her dinner.

She took the first bite of her burger and closed her eyes, sighing with absolute pleasure. It was much better than she'd even imagined. A literal taste of freedom. She chewed slowly, savoring the experience and everything it represented for her.

Her last meal, he'd called it. He'd been joking, but it was true enough to her. Her first and last night on her own, making her own choices. Except she wasn't really. *He* was here.

She blinked back the tears that were forming in her eyes and took another bite. She sighed again, relishing the flavor. Relishing freedom. All she would ever have was a taste, before she was shipped off to marry a man she didn't know. A man she didn't love or even have a special attraction to. And she was prepared to do that— had been her entire life. Was prepared to face her duty for the sake of her country. But she'd wanted time out from it all first. She hadn't thought it was too much to hope for. Apparently it had been.

Now the food felt dry in her mouth and heavy in her stomach.

"Isabella?"

She looked up, and her eyes locked with Adham's. Being the subject of his intense focus made her insides feel jittery. She didn't like being on the receiving end of that dark, knowing gaze. It was as if he could see into her, into every private thought and feeling she'd ever had.

She lowered her eyes, staring hard at her food. Anything to keep from showing him just how much he unnerved her. She was used to being at an advantage, used

to being royalty and feeling like it. But it didn't seem
to matter to this man at all. There was no deference to-
wards her position, not even the semblance of respect
she was used to receiving from strangers by virtue of
her status.

"You are thinking hard, Isabella."

She looked up at him. He flexed his hand, curled it
into a fist as if he'd been seized by sudden tension.

"Your emotions are easy to read," he said finally.

"There are two months until the wedding," she said,
trying to cultivate her best vulnerable expression, trying
to appeal to him in some way. If her emotions were easy
to read, she would use everything she had. "Two months
and ten days. I haven't gotten to do anything I planned
to do. I've never been to the cinema, or to a restaurant.
I just want…I want something of life—my own life—
before I…I get married." She watched his face, hoping
to see some expression of sympathy, a sign he was at
least hearing her words. She got nothing but that coal-
black impenetrable stare. She could feel the wall between
them, feel the distance he'd placed so efficiently between
them.

She pressed on, her heart beating faster. "Could you…?
Why couldn't I do some of the things I planned, only *with*
you?"

This at least earned her a small response, in the form
of a fractional lift of his eyebrow. "I am not a babysitter,
amira." The Arabic word for princess was tinged with
mockery.

"And I'm not a baby."

"I am here to bring you to your fiancé, and that is
where our association begins and ends. After you've been
to see the Eiffel Tower tomorrow we will fly back to

Umarah. You will go to the palace there, and then I will leave you in the capable hands of the High Sheikh."

"But…" She was stalled by the look on his face, the blank hardness that conveyed both disinterest and contempt with ruthless efficiency. She took another bite of her hamburger and tried not to cry. Not in front of him. She wasn't going to confirm what he thought—that she was some silly child who didn't know what was best for her own life.

Although that was half true. She *didn't* know. She realized that. How could she possibly know what was best for herself if she had no idea who she really was? She didn't know her own likes, her own dislikes, her own moral code. She only knew what she'd been *told* she liked. What she'd been *told* was best for her. How could she go to a strange country, with customs entirely different from any she was familiar with, marry a man she didn't know, if she still didn't know herself? What would be left of her when she was stripped away from everything she knew?

When her surroundings changed, when the people who chose her clothing, dictated her actions changed, she was terrified she might lose herself completely. That was just one reason she needed some time to find out more about herself on her own terms.

Her throat felt tighter. It felt as if everything was closing in on her. The room, her family's expectations. This was why she'd left in the first place. It was why she couldn't stay now.

She took a deep breath and made an effort to smile. She had a limited amount of time to form a plan, and she couldn't sacrifice her head start by tipping him off to what she was thinking.

"I'm tired," she said. It was true. She was so tired she

felt heavy with it. But she didn't have the luxury of collapsing yet.

"You can sleep in the guest bedroom." He gestured to a doorway that was situated across the open living room. She put her half-eaten dinner back on the wax paper, sad that she hadn't been able to enjoy it more, and stood, making a move to grab her pink suitcase.

Adham reached over and put his hand on the suitcase. Over hers. The heat singed her, blazed through her body. It shocked her that his touch could be so hot.

"I'll get it," he said, standing. He kept his hand on hers, though and the warm weight was comforting and disturbing at the same time. "That's called chivalry, not servitude."

Her face felt warm, and it seemed as if her pulse was beating in her head. "I didn't know you considered yourself chivalrous."

His dark eyes clashed with hers. She pulled her hand away, shocked at the steady burn that continued even without his touch.

"Generally speaking, I don't. Would you like to call your parents? Let them know you have not been kidnapped?"

"No." She felt mildly guilty for not wanting to speak to them. But she also felt angry. She wasn't certain she could even speak to her father without everything—all the repressed frustration she felt—flooding out of her. He could have let her have this time—realized how important it was. But he hadn't.

The slight hitch of his eyebrow let her know that he disapproved. Well, fine. He could handle *his* parents the way he wanted, and she would handle hers her way.

Adham set the suitcase down just inside the door of the guest bedroom, not placing a foot inside. "I will call them, then. There's a bathroom just through that door. If you need anything, I will see that you are provided for."

She tried to force a smile. "When does the jailer make the rounds?"

His dark eyes narrowed. "You think you suffer, Isabella? You're here in this penthouse and you think yourself in prison? You are to go from being Princess of Turan to Sheikha of Umarah and that seems lacking to you? You are nothing more than a selfish child."

His words pounded in her head as he turned and walked away. How was it selfish to want some time for herself before she gave it all up for king and country? Sheikh and country? Why was it so wrong for her to want something—anything beyond what had been given to her by her well-meaning handlers? Because that was what it felt like. As though everyone in her life was directing her, guiding her. Forcing her. She knew her place. But she didn't have to like it. And she was not going to let Adham bring guilt on her head for seizing what little time was available to her.

It was after midnight when Isabella was certain Adham was no longer awake. Waiting had been nearly impossible. She'd been lying in the plush bed, the only thing in the penthouse that wasn't hard and modern, trying not to give in to the extreme exhaustion she felt. It had been twenty-four hours since she'd last slept, but the high of her escape from her brother's Italian villa, coupled with her first day of freedom, had been enough to keep her from sleeping on the train and then when she'd gotten into the hotel room.

He had to be asleep by now—and she had to go now,

or she wouldn't have a chance to get far enough ahead of him. Sleep, for her, would have to wait.

She got out from under the covers, still fully dressed down to her shoes, and walked as quietly as she could across the room. She picked her suitcase up and took a deep breath. No point in wasting time. The faster she got out, the better.

She cracked open the bedroom door and scanned the darkened living room. She didn't see him, and across the way there was no light coming from under his door. She said a quick, silent prayer before making her way to the front door, turning the deadbolts and letting herself out. She closed it silently behind her, and took a moment to catch her breath to calm her raging heartbeat.

Her second escape attempt in as many days.

The hallway suddenly seemed endless, the world extremely open. Her options were timed, but with that time she would grab hold of what freedom she could. And maybe she could find a way to satisfy that yearning ache inside her—that relentless thing that ate at her, made her so conscious of all of the emptiness that just seemed to sit there inside of her.

Other people had their whole lives to figure out what to do about it; their futures stretching wide before them, the unknown an exciting and beautiful thing. She had two months. Her future ended abruptly on Umarahn soil, with a title, expectations, and a husband who would be a total stranger. But she would have her time until then, and it would be her own. Not Hassan's. Not Adham's.

Her determination renewed, she walked to the elevator and pressed the button for the ground floor. In just a few moments she was down on the boulevard, dodging raindrops. Streetlamps reflected off the pooling water. Despite the late hour there were still people milling around, sitting at café tables, standing beneath awnings, talking, laughing, kissing.

It was the real world. And it was finally within reach—along with the keys to her identity.

She began to scan the darkened streets for a taxi. She wasn't sure where she would take it when she found one, but she had quite a bit of cash on hand, so she imagined she could cover a lot of ground in the space of a few hours.

A hand clamped onto her arm, fingers biting into her flesh like a vice as she was pulled into an alleyway between the penthouse and the *boulangerie* next to it. She opened her mouth to scream, but one of her attacker's arms locked like a steel bar across her chest, bringing her tight against a hard, warm body. Her assailant's other hand clamped over her mouth and stopped her shriek before any sound could emerge.

She looked around wildly, trying to see if any of the people who lingered on the street had seen. No one had. She struggled impotently. The strong body behind her didn't even move as she kicked and thrashed, spraying muddy water from the puddles into the air, throwing all her weight into her attempt to gain freedom. She might as well have been struggling against solid stone.

"Your manners leave a lot to be desired." The sound of Adham's familiar, faintly accented voice made her sag with relief. For a moment.

She swore violently in Italian—very colorful and inappropriate words she'd learned from her brother, muffled by Adham's hold.

"Will you keep quiet if I remove my hand?" His tone had an edge to it—anger, extreme annoyance, and something else that she couldn't place.

She nodded, and he let his hand fall away from her mouth but kept his arms around her.

He held her tightly against his solid body. She tried to wiggle out of his hold and his arms tightened, making her extremely conscious of all the hardened muscle of his body. All that finely honed masculinity. For a moment she could only be fascinated by the feel of him, by each and every minute difference between the male and female body.

Her breasts felt heavier, and she could feel her nipples tightening against the silken fabric of her bra. Her pulse beat heavily. In her neck, her head, down to the apex of her thighs.

"Do you have any idea what you're asking for?" he asked, his voice rough.

No. She truly didn't. Her body was asking for, craving, more of his touch. But she didn't have a clue as to why. Why she wanted to lean into his strength rather than struggle against it. Why she wanted his arms to stay locked around her. Why she wanted more of the sweet languor that was spreading through her.

"You're asking to be *killed*," he growled. Clearly he was letting the subject of their mutual attraction drop. "I could have been anyone. You're walking around out here in the middle of the night with designer luggage. You *look* as wealthy as you are. Worse, you look as ridiculously naive as you are. You're asking to be robbed. Or worse."

"I didn't…I didn't think of that." Logically, she knew crime rates in urban areas were much higher than in the small island nation she was from. But the thought had never crossed her mind. Her only thought had been escaping Adham. She'd set out to prove a point about her ability to look out for herself, and she'd done a spectacular job of not thinking it through.

He turned her so that she was facing him, her arms still pinned tightly to her sides. His hands held her steady, preventing her from running.

"What do you think you're going to do with all this freedom you seek, Isabella? You have no job, no skills. You are so naive you shouldn't be allowed to cross the street on your own!"

His words hurt. They hurt because, as much as she hated to acknowledge the truth in them, it was there. He was right. She'd never had a job. She didn't know how to go about getting one. Or an apartment. She didn't know how to drive. She had a lot of knowledge, but all that had come from books. She had never had to apply the things she'd learned to anything real or practical.

"I can find something to do," she said, pushing her reservations to one side.

"With a body like that there will be many men willing to help. For a price." His eyes raked over her, hot, glittering. There was nothing passive in those black depths— not now. There was only fire.

She struggled against him. "Let go of me." She needed to get away from him. It wasn't about the broader scope, the two months of freedom. Now it was all zeroed in on getting out of his hold—away from him and the strange electric feelings that were zinging through her system.

A man who was walking by the alley turned toward them. His expression, barely visible in the light of the lamp he stood under, was concerned.

Adham backed her up a few steps, so that she rested against the brick wall of the *boulangerie*, and before she could protest his mouth was covering hers, his tongue sliding against the seam of her lips, requesting entry. She gave it.

Her mind was blank of everything but the feeling of his lips on hers. His hands roaming from her hips to her waist, to the swell of her breasts. She gripped his shoulders, steadying herself, grateful for the wall of the building behind her and the wall of his body in front. If not for those things she would have melted into one of the rain puddles at his feet.

He pulled away suddenly, his breathing harsh in the stillness of the night air. Isabella touched her lips, confirming that they were as swollen as they felt.

"What…?" she breathed, unable to speak any more coherently than that.

"It's Paris," he bit out. "No one is going to interrupt lovers. Even if they are having a disagreement."

He took her arm and led her out of the shadows and back toward the main door of his building. Her rage mingled with something else—something hot and dangerous and completely unsettling. She put a hand to her mouth again, to confirm she hadn't hallucinated the entire event.

When they were back in the building he propelled her into the lift, the doors shut behind them. She couldn't believe he had done that. Kissed her as though he had every right to touch her, as though he…he had some *claim* on her. And only to shut her up. Her first kiss had been a diversion.

Worse than all of that, she couldn't believe the restless ache that was building in her body. The curiosity. The need to know what it would be like to kiss him again. Only this time longer and gentler, slowly so she had time to process it, to learn the texture of his lips, the rhythm of his movements.

She shut that traitorous part of her brain down. He'd had no right to do that. She wore another man's ring. Even in her wildest fantasies of escape she had never imagined betraying her fiancé in that way. She didn't know the man. She certainly didn't love him. But they had a signed agreement, and she had no intention of violating it.

He'd done it to shut her up. That stung her pride. Much more than it should.

"I can't believe you did that," she said icily.

He looked at her, his dark eyes unreadable, his lips—lips that had just claimed hers with what had felt like hunger—now pressed into a flat, immovable line. There was no passion there. He was unaffected. A man made of cold, unyielding stone.

"If you learn one thing about me learn this, and learn it quickly," he said, his voice hard. "I will do whatever it takes to ensure my objective is met. I intend to take you back to Sheikh Hassan, and I will do it."

She believed him. Her scarred captor with the fathomless eyes was most certainly capable of getting his way. Of seeing that she didn't get hers. She felt as if she'd stepped into water, expecting a wading pool, only to find she had swum out into the middle of an ocean. Out of her depth didn't begin to describe it.

She walked from the lift back into the penthouse, and tried not to imagine a barred cell door swinging shut when Adham closed the door behind them.

"How did you know? How did you get down there so fast?"

"I was expecting it. I deal with masterminds, Isabella, one naive princess is not going to pull one over on me. There's an alarm on the door that's linked to my mobile phone, and the stairs are faster than the elevator."

She closed her eyes against mounting anguish, tried

to fight the tears that were threatening. She didn't want to dissolve in front of him. Didn't want him to see how defeated she felt. How could a man who was allowed to do whatever he wanted, a man who roamed the world, lived by his own rules, possibly understand the preciousness of two months and ten days worth of freedom?

She looked at his hardened face, the scars. Appealing to him for a show of kindness would be like attempting to squeeze water from a rock. It was impossible. You couldn't extract what wasn't there.

"Go to bed, Isabella." His voice was as hard as everything else about him.

She felt as if she was going to break, but she wouldn't do it in front of him.

She nodded jerkily and stumbled into her bedroom, closing the door behind her with a click.

Adham stalked across the room and retrieved his phone from the coffee table, hitting the speed dial for his brother, not caring what time it was in their home country.

"*Salaam*, brother," Adham said curtly.

"*Salaam*," Hassan returned the greeting, his tone questioning. "You've found Isabella?"

"I have found your wayward fiancée, as requested."

"And she is well?"

"She is uninjured, if that's what you mean. But she did make another escape attempt."

"She's unhappy?" His brother sounded genuinely concerned.

"She is a spoiled child. She has no reason to be so discontent. She wants for nothing."

Hassan sighed heavily into the phone. "I regret that she is reluctant about the marriage. But it's a much needed alliance, and marriage is the best way to seal such bargains. It is necessary insurance in something so critical."

"I understand the reason for your union. But I find her childish."

"You do not think she will make a suitable bride?"

"I will gladly hand her over to you and see that she becomes your problem as quickly as possible."

Hassan laughed. "You make me eager for her to arrive." He paused for a moment. "Is there nothing that can be done to make her happy? A gift, perhaps? A ring that is more to her liking?"

"She wants to see the Eiffel Tower," Adham bit out in response.

"Simple enough."

"She has some idea that she is lacking in life experience. She intends to go and find herself some *experience*."

There was another pause on the other end of the line. "The wedding is not for two more months, Adham. If that is what she wants, I see no reason why you can't accommodate her—so long as the experience she seeks is not in a man's bed."

There was something different in his brother's tone. A desperation he had not heard before. Adham had the feeling that his request had little to do with Isabella, but he would not ask.

"I am not a babysitter." He repeated his earlier words. "Have one of your other men come and watch over her while she tries to play at living her spoiled princess fantasy of what real life is."

"I don't have that kind of trust in anyone else. Another man would be too tempted by her. I'm certain that you've noticed she's an incredibly beautiful woman."

He'd noticed. It was difficult not to. She had the sort

of beauty that no red-blooded man could ignore. And he didn't want to spend any more time with her than was necessary.

"You will keep her safe?" Hassan pressed.

"You have my word. On my honor, I will keep her from harm. I will keep her untouched." His vow was from the heart. He served Hassan always. Gladly. Hassan was his only family, and there was no bond stronger than that forged in blood.

"I have absolute faith in you, Adham," his brother continued. "You will keep her safe and make her happy. It will ease my conscience."

"As you will it," Adham ground out, before ending the call.

He tossed the phone onto the couch and tried to calm his raging pulse. At the moment he felt like a fox that had just been asked to guard the henhouse.

Kissing her had been a miscalculation on his part. He had not anticipated his body's reaction to such a simple thing. He had far too much experience for a mere kiss to fire his blood.

And yet kissing Isabella had done just that. His body was still hard, and a dark, physical need was gripping him. There was no denying that in a physical sense he desired her. And she was the one woman he was forbidden to touch.

But it was a simple matter of control. And once he had made his decision he would not deviate from it. He never did.

CHAPTER THREE

ISABELLA surfaced quietly the next morning, creeping out of the sparsely furnished bedroom and into the main living area. Her eyes were puffy from crying and from lack of sleep. But the moments of indulgence had been worth it in a way. And now she was done with feeling sorry for herself.

She pulled her thick hair up into a ponytail and walked through the expansive living room and into the kitchen. She took an apple out of a fruit bowl on the counter and sat down at the small dining table.

Adham strode into the room a moment later, his crisp white shirt open at the collar, revealing a V of golden muscular chest. His black hair was wet and curling around the neck of his shirt. He smelled fresh, clean and wholly male, his natural scent spiked with a hint of sandalwood—exotic, spicy, and completely erotic. She couldn't remember ever noticing the scent of a man before. Her father's cologne, her brother's aftershave, but never the scent that was beneath the product. She noticed it now. It made her lungs feel tight, as if she couldn't bring in enough air.

She placed the apple on the table. "Good morning."

He gave her a skeptical look, one that told her he quite plainly disagreed, and jerked the refrigerator door open, turning his attention to hunting for food. "Have you eaten?"

She shook her head mutely, before realizing that he couldn't see her. "No. I just got up."

"Late nights prowling the street do tend to make one tired."

She gritted her teeth to bite back all the angry words that were swirling in her head, all the justification and excuses. None of it would matter to him. As far as he was concerned she was simply a package for him to deliver. "So I'm discovering."

He closed the fridge abruptly and straightened, training his dark, impenetrable gaze on her. "Never endanger yourself like that again, Isabella. You do not understand how dangerous the world is. How can you?"

"I live surrounded by bodyguards. I understand that life is dangerous."

"Do you? Because you did not seem like a woman who understood that last night."

"I didn't really imagine that the neighborhood around your upscale penthouse would pose a danger."

"Danger can be anywhere. Even in the most luxurious surroundings. Especially there."

The dark note in his voice told her he spoke from an experience she couldn't begin to understand. His scars ran deep. Those on the surface were only a glimpse of what was beneath. But it didn't repel her. It only made her curious about the man who was the Sheikh's most trusted employee. The man who seemed to have no fear for himself, yet feared for her safety.

He took her apple from its spot on the table and placed it back in the fruit bowl. "Let's go to a café. You can see more of the city."

Wariness along with a small surge of hope flared to life inside her. "I thought you didn't babysit."

"I don't. Consider this your guided tour of life."

"What changed your mind?" she asked, apprehension combining with excitement now, and her stomach tightening with anticipation.

"It has nothing to do with me. It's what Hassan wants. If it were up to me you would be on a plane to Umarah right now and would no longer be my problem. But your future husband has seen fit to allow you to have your *life experiences*. Within reason, of course."

She imagined it was what prisoners might feel like when they found out that their execution date had been pushed back. It was a reprieve, but the execution still loomed. And she would be living her remaining days with her jailer as her constant companion. But she wouldn't let herself think of what would happen after her time in Paris. This was about her. She deserved it. Deserved to have some time devoted to things that interested her. Some time devoted to discovering what things interested her.

"Thank you," she choked out, the lump in her throat keeping her from speaking more. She closed the distance between them, wrapped her arms around his neck.

Adham stood rigid, his arms pinned tightly to his sides. He was unwilling to do so much as breathe, for fear his control would slip even more and he would give in to the ache of arousal that was pounding heavily through his body.

He could not remember the last time a woman, or anyone for that matter, had hugged him. Clung to him, kissed him, rubbed her body against him in invitation— sure. But just a hug—a show of warmth, of affection, an innocent gesture... He didn't know if he had ever experienced that. He had been so long without his family, so long without frequent, human contact, that he could not remember any more what it had been like. Since the death of his parents it had only been Hassan and himself, and neither of them were given to overt displays of affection.

"I do not want your gratitude," he said, pulling away from her hold, ignoring the tightness in his body. Ignoring what it meant. "This was not my doing."

Her eyes widened, and hurt evident in their blue depths—as though she was a child responding to being scolded. Such a contradiction. She was a woman, not a child, but she seemed to switch roles with ease. A woman when it suited her to be enticing. A sweet innocent when she wanted sympathy. It was a façade, an act, and though it was effective it would not work on him.

She bit her lip and looked down, the crease between her dark, perfectly shaped brows deepening, as if to show contrition. "I'm sorry. But this is the only chance I'll have to…to figure out who I am. I don't know if someone like you could understand."

"Someone like me?" he asked, mildly amused that she'd clearly taken him to be nothing more than a body-guard.

"Someone who's had freedom his whole life. Someone who's had the ability to make his own decisions. I haven't had that chance. It's…it's more than that. I don't know if I can fully explain it. I just know that I need to be able to have some experiences of my own."

He crossed his arms over his chest, unmoved by her speech. "And what is at the top of this list of yours?"

She raised her eyes again, a glimmer of excitement there now. "I want to do things I haven't done before. Go to the movies. A club, maybe?"

"Not a club," he said flatly.

If she went to a club every heterosexual male in the area would be all over her. Given her sheltered upbringing, she likely had no clue what kind of effect a body like hers had on men. She'd played at flirting with him, but playing was all it had been. In that sort of environment she would be like a lamb that had wandered into a wolf pack.

"Okay, not a club," she said, not looking at all dented by his refusal. "But definitely the Eiffel Tower, the Champs-Élysées, a restaurant. And *definitely* shopping."

"Get dressed. I'll take you to breakfast."

Isabella took a long sip of her espresso and followed it up with a bite of pastry. She closed her eyes and moaned.

The burn that hit him hot and hard in his stomach, along with the slow flood of blood that went south of his belt, made him tense.

He hadn't noticed before what a sensual person Isabella was. Watching her eat a pastry and drink coffee, listening to the sounds she made—small kitten moans in the back of her throat—watching the way she closed her eyes as if she was in ecstasy, seeing her lick each remaining crumb from her full lips, was erotic torture.

The only thing that matched the arousal racing through his system was the growing disgust that had settled in his gut. She was his brother's woman. She was forbidden. He should not want her, should not touch her, should not look at her as a man looked at a woman. And yet he found himself looking. Wanting. But he would never touch her. *Not again.* That time in the alley, when his lips had met hers, it had been necessary. It was a moment that would never be repeated.

He would not betray his brother in such a manner.

The loyalty that existed between them was not something that could be thrown aside for a mere woman. The bond between himself and his brother had always been strong, but after the death of their parents that link between them had been strengthened. Hassan had devoted his life to ruling Umarah, guiding their people, forging diplomatic alliances and handling the delicate matters of state. Adham's life was devoted to protecting Hassan, to guarding their people. They were a right and a left hand. Hassan had been the public ruler from the time their parents had died, but they functioned as a team, working with their strengths for the betterment of their people.

There would be no compromising that.

"This place is amazing. Like a fantasy."

She inhaled deeply, and his eyes were drawn to the shape of her rounded breasts pushing against her top.

Clearly her fantasies were different from his. But then, that was to be expected. Another reminder of why she was not the sort of woman who should arouse his libido. Even if his brother weren't a factor. She was an innocent. A virgin. He had never touched a virgin and never would as he didn't ever intend to take a wife.

"Paris can hardly be beaten for atmosphere, although I'm partial to the desert. I like the heat, the open space, the solitude."

Her smooth forehead creased. "I've never been to the desert. I can't really imagine it being beautiful. Whenever I envision the desert I see cactuses and bleached bones."

"It's not an easy beauty to see. Not like the architecture here in Paris, and not like the green mountains in Turan. It's fierce and barren—just the sand and the sky. It asks a lot of a man, but if the man can rise to the challenge, if he can learn to exist in such a place, he can't help but love it."

Her blue eyes glittered, the sudden humor there unexpected. "And you've risen to the challenge and defeated the desert?"

Her mischievous smile pulled a reluctant laugh from him. "I haven't beaten it. It's impossible to tame the desert. There are fierce sandstorms, unforgiving temperatures, and poisonous reptiles. The best you can hope is that she'll allow you a peaceful existence."

She offered him a sweet half-smile that just barely curved the edges of her full lips. "And the desert is a woman?"

"Of course she is. Only a woman could be such a fierce mistress."

"I can't imagine the kind of freedom the desert must offer," she said, after a long moment of silence.

"It's a freedom that demands responsibility. You have to respect where you are at all times. You have to keep the rules and mind the boundaries."

"And uphold duty and honor?"

"What is there in life without those things, Isabella? If men discard such notions, what keeps the world moving?"

Isabella hated how right he was. Hated that what he said made so much sense. She understood the importance of her alliance with Hassan, High Sheikh of Umarah. It was good for the economy, good for building a strong bond between nations in case of any sort of crisis. And if it weren't her life, if she were only a casual observer like Adham, who wasn't the one being forced to marry a stranger, she would have felt as he did.

But it was her life. Not some vague idea of honor and duty. She was the sacrificial lamb for the masses. Easy for him to speak that way when in the end he got to ride off into the sunset and be with whom he wished, doing whatever he wished.

"I have accepted the path I have to take, Adham," she said, trying to keep her voice from wobbling. "I only wanted to take a small detour."

"And where would you like your detour to take you now, Princess?" His voice was hard. Condescending. A sharp contrast to the small moment of near camaraderie they'd just shared.

Well, fine. She didn't much care for him either.

"I thought we could walk. See the sights."

He nodded in what she assumed was acquiescence. He had a way of making her feel as though he disapproved with nothing more than the slightest movement. Even though he'd agreed, the tension in his body told her he'd rather do anything else. Not the most accommodating man, her keeper.

He turned and began to walk up the boulevard, not getting too far ahead of her, but not exactly waiting for her either. She knew that no matter what it seemed like his focus was still on her. She knew it because her skin felt too tight and her stomach was queasy with knots.

She quickened her pace, taking two steps to his one, her much shorter legs making her work harder to gain the distance he was managing. She looked around at the tourists pouring from buses that lined the sidewalks. They were in groups. Pairs. Holding hands. Why did it suddenly seem as though it would be natural to be linked to Adham in that way? To hold his hand while they strolled through Paris together?

She fell into step beside him and her hand brushed his. Her heart leapt to her throat at the contact. He didn't even look at her. Didn't give her any indication that he had noticed her touch, let alone been affected by it.

Except she noticed him curling his hand tightly into a fist, the tendons shifting, the scars on his skin lightening as he squeezed tightly before relaxing it again. She rubbed the back of her own hand idly, her skin still hot from his touch. Maybe his skin was hot from the brush of her hand too?

She looked at him again, at his hard, immobile face, so perfect it seemed to be etched in stone. The marks on his skin were evidence of time and living rather than a detraction to his masculine beauty. An addition to the form the artist had wrought, showing the character of the man, of all he had endured.

No. It was impossible that she'd manage to have any effect on a man like him. He was quite incredibly out of her league, in more ways than she could count. She didn't know how old he was, but she was certain he was quite a bit older than her own twenty-one. Add his experience and living to that, and it seemed they were from different worlds.

That realization made an uncomfortable weight settle in her stomach. He probably didn't take her any more seriously than if she were a child whining for an ice cream cone.

She shook her head. It didn't matter what Adham thought of her. He didn't have to live her life. *She did.* She looked over the tops of the tour buses, past the neatly shorn trees that were carefully crafted into tall hedges, at the top of the Eiffel Tower, visible above all of it.

They reached the end of the row of foliage and the full tower came into view. People were everywhere, snapping photographs of the intricate scaffolding and of each other.

She wondered how she and her stoic companion must look to them.

She noticed very quickly that women were all but giving themselves whiplash with extreme head-turns when Adham walked by. Pride warred with another more uncomfortable emotion. Pride because he was the best looking man even in this densely populated spot, and he was with *her*. But the other feeling, the one that made her stomach ache, was not welcome.

"Would you take my picture?" she asked, fishing for the small digital camera she'd tucked into her purse before leaving her brother's home and holding it out to him. She wanted memories. Reminders of the time when she'd been free to make her own choices.

He raised his dark eyebrow at her, clearly less than pleased to be playing tourist.

Another feeling roiled in her stomach, and this one she knew for sure. Anger. "Please. Just take my picture and stop acting like you're here under sufferance."

She caught a small, barely detectable curving of his lips. "I *am* here under sufferance." But he took the camera from her outstretched hand.

She positioned herself in front of the lawn and smiled wide. Suddenly she wished she were taking *his* picture. His face would be compelling on film. His masculine bone structure, his scarred golden skin. Maybe if she had a photo she could look at his dark eyes long enough to read his secrets.

He snapped the picture and she jumped, realizing she'd been somewhere else entirely. That wasn't right. She needed to be living in the moment. She was at the Eiffel Tower, in Paris. No looking ahead, no looking back, and no looking into Adham's eyes. He was just an unfortunate accessory to her trip, nothing more.

"Did it turn out okay?" she asked.

He looked at the small screen, his expression tight. "It's fine." He walked to her and thrust the camera back into her hand, his manner abrupt. Nothing new there. Was there any way to penetrate that wall he had up? Was there a woman, one he loved, that those dark eyes softened for?

The thought made her feel nauseous. She didn't want to think about the woman who got to see past his defenses. But if she were to try and imagine that woman she pictured her being older, sophisticated—not just in the sense of having an affluent upbringing, but savvy in the ways of the world. Knowledgeable of things Isabella was hardly aware of.

She would certainly be the opposite of Isabella, since the only thing she seemed to arouse in Adham was extreme annoyance.

"Ready?" he asked, his voice clipped.

No, she wasn't ready. But she doubted it really mattered. "Sure."

Her pique was forgotten as they walked through the city, past beautiful stone architecture and historic sites. She lingered in one of the narrow streets, taking photographs of a rustic wooden door painted a rich, saturated blue. She wanted to capture it forever, to remember the simple moment of unexpected beauty and color amidst the monochromatic grays.

"It's a door, Isabella." Adham's bored voice sent a shiver of irritation and tension through her.

"Yes, it is, Adham. A blue one. Glad your gift of observation is so well-honed. It's little wonder you're such an indispensable member of the Umarahn guard."

He captured her arm, gently but firmly, and turned

her so that she was facing him. "I am not a member of the Umarahn guard. I *am* the Umarahn guard."

He was so close. Like he'd been in the alley. It was so easy to imagine him pulling her to him, capturing her lips again.

She moved away. "They're lucky to have you."

She walked ahead of him this time, keeping her eyes locked in front of her. She didn't know why his comment had bothered her so much. Maybe because she'd seen beauty in that simple thing and it had meant something to her to try and capture that. Something that had felt important. And he hadn't seen it at all. Not that it should matter.

The alleyway spilled out onto a busier street, lined with shops and cafés, and further down the massive Printemps department store.

She felt a renewed flaring of excitement. "Can we go shopping?"

"Shopping? Does that rate as an important, life-altering experience for you?"

Mild irritation gave way to seething anger. "I don't know. Maybe it does. I haven't really been before. At least not without the aid of my mother's personal shopper, telling me what is and isn't appropriate. But you wouldn't understand that. You take for granted your God-given free will because no one's stolen it from you."

"And you think these shallow experiences will teach you something of life? It shows how little you know, Isabella. You see only what's been denied you, not what you've been protected from." His dark eyes burned into her, making her feel exposed, as though all her inadequacies were revealed to him. "Not all experiences are good."

She swallowed hard. "You speak as a man who has never been a prisoner."

He took a step toward her and she stepped back, dodging a pedestrian. "I *have* been a prisoner. A prisoner of war. Where do you think these came from?" He indicated the marks etched into his cheek. "You are nothing more than a foolish child. You know nothing of the world. Be grateful for that."

CHAPTER FOUR

ISABELLA flicked her eyes up and focused on Adham's cool expression, reflected in the dressing room mirror. "You don't like it?"

He shrugged, his expression one of cool disinterest. "Buy what *you* like."

She fixed her gaze back on her reflection. Yes. She was going to buy what *she* liked. It didn't matter what he thought, or what her mother's personal shopper would say. The only thing that mattered was how she felt about the outfit. The crisp white button-up top hugged her breasts and nipped in at the waist, accentuating her hourglass shape, while the brown satin shorts showed off more of her golden legs than she was accustomed to. But she thought she looked nice. She was reasonably certain she looked nice.

She looked back at Adham. "Is it unflattering?"

His coal-dark eyes raked over her, and it made her want to tug on the wide cuff of the shorts so that she could get some more coverage. "It's very flattering."

Isabella was suddenly conscious of the fact that they were alone in the dressing area. Her skin felt sensitized. She could feel the air touching her, closing in on her. She could feel Adham's heat across the small space.

"Th-thank you." Her heart was beating harder now,

her palms damp. She needed…she needed distance. She didn't want to be closed in with Adham anymore, didn't want to share the air with him. Air that suddenly seemed thicker, harder to breathe. "So…so you like it, then?" She despised the hopeful tone in her voice.

His Adam's apple bobbed; his eyes flickering over her curves. "I like it."

She noticed that he tightened his hands into fists again, then released them, flexing his long, masculine fingers.

He was the most infuriating man. He'd all but crushed her before they'd gone into Printemps, making her feel like a silly child, and now, only half an hour later, he was making her more conscious of the fact that she was a woman than she'd ever been before.

"I'm finished," she said tightly, disappearing into the dressing room and putting on her own clothes as quickly as possible, before exiting with her carefully chosen outfits.

She added the packages to the shoes she'd purchased already, which included a pair of very sexy, strappy high-heeled sandals and tall butter-soft brown leather boots. Definitely not things her mother's personal shopper would have chosen.

They meandered through the massive department store, and Isabella did her best to simply block out everything but the moment she was living in. She loved being surrounded by the crowd of people, by the low hum of conversation. She was *with* people rather than above them—a part of things rather than held back, kept separate from everyone.

Although Adham seemed content to hold himself separate on purpose. From her, from everyone. Though he wore designer jeans and a T-shirt with ease, he seemed

out of place in their urban surroundings. He stood out—
his height, his breadth, his handsome features, his scars
all drawing attention to him. But it was more than just
his looks. He seemed too exotic, too wild for something
as prosaic as a department store.

He was so completely unaffected. By the sights, by
the crowds, by her. And he was making her feel edgy and
restless and…nervous. He was definitely affecting her, no
matter how much she was trying to pretend otherwise.

With a spark of defiance she checked the map of the
large store that she was carrying with her and headed to
the lingerie floor. That was another part of her wardrobe
that needed dragging into the contemporary era. She had
lovely underwear, it was true. The highest quality. But the
styles gave no concession to a woman's sexuality—which
had always been fine with her, since she hadn't given
much thought to hers. But this was about self-discovery,
and she was not changing dictators without discovering what her personal preference in undergarments was.
If she wanted ultra-sexy panties she was going to get
them.

And Adham was coming with her. Like it or not. He
was doing a decent job of making her uncomfortable.
She might as well return the favor.

Of course her boldness nearly deserted her when they
reached the lingerie floor. She looked at Adham out of
the corner of her eye and noticed him clenching his fist
again. He did that a lot. She was convinced it meant
that he was uncomfortable. Good. He deserved some
discomfort. His presence was one big giant discomfort
in her behind, so a little turnabout seemed like fair play
to her.

"I'd like to look around here for a while," she said,
trying to keep her expression as neutral as possible.

Adham's eyes darkened, his jaw clenched tight along with his fist. "If you wish."

"You could wait in one of the cafés." But she knew he wouldn't.

"I don't think that would be wise."

She took a deep breath and tried to look casual—tried to look as if having a man with her while she looked at intimate items of clothing was both normal and no big deal at all. "All right."

She moved to one of the display tables and began to pick out the smallest, filmiest panties she could find, and thongs—something her mother never would have allowed her even to look at. She would think they were the sort of undergarments only suited to women of questionable moral character. A surge of power coursed through Isabella as she selected one thong in each pattern and color available, every one briefer, more revealing than the last.

It didn't matter if her mother would have disapproved of them. It was her decision to make. The very fact that there were people in her life who controlled what she wore beneath her clothing was sad beyond belief. But that would change. Even when she went to Umarah she would not allow that to be dictated to her. Not anymore.

Of course she would want to wear them only in her own chambers. She couldn't possibly imagine wearing them for her future husband. She didn't even know the man.

That thought made her want to throw all the revealing items down and run out of the store. But she wouldn't do that. This was about her. About what she wanted. Not what anyone else wanted or didn't want.

She finally sneaked a glance at Adham, who had fallen quite a bit behind her. She noticed his dark eyes were burning with intensity, his hands locked so tightly that the scars were bright white against a backdrop of golden skin.

She was getting to him. Pleasure uncurled in her belly, winding through her. Pride that she might hold enough appeal for him that she was capable of making him uneasy.

With a sudden surge of confidence she sauntered to the negligees. The selection was phenomenal—silks, sheers, pale pinks and electric blues. And every style was sexier than anything she'd ever seen, let alone been permitted to own. She didn't see why she should be confined to floor-length nightgowns. She was twenty-one, for heaven's sake, and she still had nightwear in the same style she'd worn at the all-girls boarding school she'd attended seven years ago.

She picked up a gauzy peach babydoll-style nightie that would barely cover the tops of her thighs. The Grecian pleating over the cups wouldn't be sufficient to cover her breasts—not when the fabric was nearly see-through. The glass beads sewn beneath the bustline looked sinful, somehow. Decadent. She loved it.

A wicked impulse seized her and she turned to face Adham, holding the negligee up so he could get a good look at it. "How about this? Do you think it would be flattering?"

Adham's face remained as coolly impassive as ever, a slight tightening of his jaw the only indication that he'd heard her. He began to walk toward her, the heat in his eyes causing an answering fire to ignite low in her belly.

He was so close, too close, his masculine scent teasing her, making her heart pound heavily. She tried to swallow, but her throat felt as if it was coated in sandpaper.

He extended his hand and ran his fingers along the edge of the nightie's neckline, his callused fingers abrading the delicate fabric, the sound sending a faint shiver through her. His eyes were locked with hers, the dark intensity in them robbing her of the ability to breathe.

He slid his fingers down over the negligee, his thumb caressing the part that would have been covering her breasts had she been wearing it.

It was far too easy to imagine those rough fingers moving over her body, imagine how his fingers would feel against her soft, tender skin. Evidence of his strength, his hard work, his character.

Her breasts suddenly felt heavy, her nipples stinging as they tightened into hard points. She was absolutely, completely disturbed by what he was making her feel. But she was also captive to it, spellbound by the power he had over her body. He could make her feel more than any fantasy or real-life person ever had without even touching her.

Her breath was caught in her throat, every nerve, every cell in her body waiting to see what he would do next.

"I don't know that it's your color," he said, his eyes never leaving hers. "You should try for something more daring."

For a moment—one heady, wonderful moment—she thought he was going to lean in and capture her lips again. He was so close. It would have been the easiest thing to close the distance between them, for her to touch her lips to his.

"A brighter shade, I think," he said, his voice rough. "Sheikh Hassan prefers women who wear vivid colors."

He stepped away from her then, his eyes flat, all the heat gone. She couldn't have been more shocked if he'd dumped a bucket of ice water over her. He'd had her spellbound, unconscious of where she was, who she was. It was a shock to find out that she was still standing in Printemps, beneath the bright lights, with other shoppers milling around them as though they weren't there.

And she was still wearing Hassan's ring.

"I like this one," she said, trying to inject authority into her voice. Difficult when she could hardly catch her breath.

She held the negligee tightly to her chest and clutched the panties in a bundled-up knot of fabric as she headed to the register to pay for her lingerie. He had been trying to put her off, but she wasn't going to let him.

She imagined he'd also been trying to show her that *he* was in control, that she was out of her depth. And that he had succeeded in, she hated to admit.

She'd felt confident enough in her knowledge of men and sex to tease him, torment him a bit as he'd been doing to her. She'd gleaned enough knowledge from her time away at school, from late-night chatting sessions with her friends, and then, more recently, from her sister-in-law Alison. But with one searing look, with the effect he'd had on her body, Adham had proved to her that she knew nothing. Nothing real, anyway.

Romance novels and jokes with friends were one thing, but actual sexual attraction, need, desire was quite another. She'd never really realized just how different the two were until she'd watched him stroke his fingers over the silken material of the nightgown. As she'd imagined him touching her in the same manner.

The thought made her hot all over.

She handed the clerk her credit card—no point being discreet now that she'd been found—and waited while her sexy new nothings were packaged into two neat little boxes with satin ribbon handles. She added those to her other shopping bags, a small feeling of accomplishment swelling in her chest.

Maybe Adham thought shopping was stupid, but she felt as if she'd claimed some small portion of her life for herself, and there was nothing stupid about that.

"Are you ready to go?" he asked, his voice rougher than normal, his accent thicker.

"I am getting hungry. But we could just eat here…"

"I have my limits on shopping," he said, his lip curled slightly. "Normally I hand women my credit card and send them on their way."

He started to walk toward the exit doors and she followed him quickly. "What? Women you date?"

He turned and looked at her for a brief moment, his dark eyebrows drawn together. "I don't know that I would call it that."

Of course not. Men like him probably had affairs. He'd probably had lots of rich lovers who reveled in having such a tough, macho man for a bedmate. Except he really didn't seem like the sort of man who would be content to be a woman's plaything. And, as he'd said, he was the one handing out credit cards.

She looked at him, her heart stuttering as she took in that broad, muscled back, his tapered waist and slim hips. Oh, no, Adham wouldn't be any woman's plaything. He was too much a man for that. He would want the upper hand in every way. He would be dominant in every situation.

Not for the first time she thought he seemed nothing like the staff at the Turani palace. He didn't defer to her. Ever. He acted like a man who was used to being in control, used to having his orders unchallenged, used to having his way. But then, he'd been in the military—likely as a leader—so it could be true.

"What would you call it, then?" she asked, curiosity demanding more than speculation.

"I don't know that I'm ever in one place long enough to date. I have arrangements."

That hot emotion stirred her stomach again, and this time she recognized it. Jealousy. Not really directed at the women, but because it was such a casual thing to him. He had *arrangements*. No one dictated to him whether or not he could have them, who he could have them with, how he conducted them.

Isabella was reasonably certain that even if she'd been given carte blanche to have relationships with men they wouldn't have been casual *arrangements*, but having the freedom would have been nice. Learning her own moral code, her own limits—that would have been nice too.

It would be nice to know her parents had that kind of trust in her.

Of course relationships hadn't been feasible, because an arranged marriage had always been a foregone conclusion. She'd been ten when it had been decided that Hassan al bin Sudar would be the man. There would never have been any point to her dating anyone. Even so, she was jealous of Adham's freedom, of the casual way he spoke of it.

"I've never had a relationship," she said, closing her eyes as they exited the store, as the cool air hit her face, the slight breeze ruffling her hair.

"You're engaged. Most people would count that as a relationship," he said, his voice tight.

"Well, most people who are engaged have met their fiancé, or at the very least selected him."

"It's different for royalty, Isabella. You know that."

"Of course I do."

Adham halted mid-stride and turned, taking her bags from her hands, his fingers brushing hers, sending a shock of heat straight to her toes. Then he turned and started walking again, as though the world hadn't just tilted a little. Although she supposed the world had remained upright as ever to him.

"What about you?" she asked, suddenly wanting to know more about her scarred guardian. "Do you ever plan to marry?"

"No."

"Just…no?"

"My life isn't suited to marriage and family. It is full. And I have no desire for a wife."

"Well, it's a good thing you aren't the High Sheikh, or you would be required to marry me."

He paused slightly, his shoulders tensing. It was a small reaction—one she would have missed if she weren't so tuned into him. "If it were required of me, I would do it."

"That's it? If it were required of you, you would change all of your expectations to fulfill your duty?"

"I would."

He said it with such certainty that she didn't doubt him. But it was easy for him. He didn't have dreams of love and romance. Even knowing she'd had an arranged marriage, part of her had always harbored fantasies of love. It was normal for women—for most people, really. Everyone wanted to be loved.

Except Adham, apparently. *He* only needed lovers. A thought that was much more intriguing than it should be. Because her thoughts had no place wandering down that road—not with Adham. Not with any man other than her chosen fiancé.

Even knowing that, when they rounded a corner and

she closed her eyes against the harsh shaft of afternoon light that shone between the tightly packed buildings, it was an imprint of Adham's face that she saw.

CHAPTER FIVE

ADHAM was taking her to the cinema, and she was unaccountably nervous. It felt like...like a date—even though the very idea was completely ridiculous. He'd all but ignored her for the past few days—conducting business in his office, checking on his oil field, making contact with other security officers, and leaving her to fend for herself.

But that morning she'd brought up the subject of the movie theater, and he'd agreed.

She'd been trying to decide on an outfit for nearly forty minutes. Which was ridiculous, because it shouldn't matter what she wore so long as *she* was happy with it. But she kept picturing Adham's face, his reaction to her, wondering if any of that smoldering heat would flare in his eyes when he saw her, and what article of clothing might help her accomplish that.

It was not a productive line of thinking. But she was wandering down the rabbit trail anyway.

She rifled through her new things and finally decided to put on the sexy crimson wrap sweater she'd purchased on their shopping excursion. The soft, clingy material hugged her curves and had a neckline that dipped low, showing just the right amount of cleavage. She decided to pair it with dark-wash jeans and some strappy heels that would no doubt make her feet ache after a few hours. But they would be worth it.

The underwear was almost as big a decision for her—which was more ridiculous than being so indecisive over the outerwear. But it mattered. Adham had seen them, had watched her purchase them. She didn't think a man had ever seen her underwear before, even when she wasn't wearing it. Knowing he would know what they looked like…the thought that he might try and guess which ones she was wearing…well, that made her feel wicked. And edgy. And just a tiny bit guilty.

She selected an ivory-colored bra, made from web-fine netting. Intricate flowers added provocative detail, framing her dusky nipples, which were clearly visible through the sheer fabric. The panties were no better—framing rather than concealing.

She looked at herself for a moment, stunned by the fact that she could look so…provocative. She'd almost entirely ignored her own sexuality because it had always seemed inextricably linked to her unknown, pre-selected future husband. But now, despite the fact that Hassan's ring was on her finger, that part of her so long denied was becoming tethered to the man who was out in the living area.

The attraction had been instantaneous. But she had been confident that once she'd spent some time with him it would diminish. It seemed as though she'd have to become accustomed to his sex appeal after all. But his appeal hadn't diminished. And her attraction was growing. Being stuck with him certainly didn't help.

She looked down at her breasts, at her nipples pushing against the gauzy fabric. She couldn't even think about him without having an actual physical reaction.

She huffed out a disgusted sound and pulled her jeans,

top and shoes on quickly. Anything to disguise that sensual image she made, standing there in her underwear. Underwear that was definitely meant to be seen.

Her mouth dropped open with shock and a mild amount of pleasure as she took in her fully dressed reflection. She'd never looked so...so outright sexy in her entire life. She turned and admired the view from the back in the mirror. Yes, she looked totally sexy. But... more than that...she looked like herself. She was different, but totally familiar. It was as if that other version of herself—the one who'd been wearing khaki slacks and a matching jacket—had been the stranger. And this was Isabella.

She stepped up to the mirror and looked at the woman staring back at her. Her make-up was lighter than the way her personal servant did it, and her hair was left natural. Loose curls tumbled past her shoulders.

For the first time she felt as though she matched her reflection. This wasn't the glossed-up princess, made to look so much older and more sophisticated than she was. This was the woman that she was inside.

She took a deep breath and got ready to go back into the main part of the penthouse. She was nervous, she realized. Because she'd only just seen herself for the first time, and now Adham would see her too—with no façade to hide behind.

She turned the handle and opened the door. Adham was sitting on the couch when she came into the main living area. His eyes were closed, his hands clasped behind his head, and his black T-shirt stretched tightly across the hard muscles of his broad chest. The sight of his tanned, toned arms made her stomach knot.

Once again she was very conscious of the fact that

he'd seen her underwear. Which was stupid. It wasn't as if he'd seen her *in* it. Or as if he'd want to.

Except when he opened his eyes and looked at her, his dark gaze taking a slow tour of her body, there was heat there. Unmistakable, undeniable heat, that burned down to her toes and every interesting spot in between.

"I'm ready," she said, aware that her voice sounded husky, affected.

The heat in his eyes intensified, and she realized her words could be interpreted to mean something different. She also realized that part of her meant them in that way.

That was wrong. Even if she wasn't happy about her engagement to Hassan, she was committed to it. The expectation was that she would go to her marriage bed a virgin—something she'd tried decently hard not to think about, if only because it was frightening to think of sharing such a momentous thing with a man she didn't love or even know.

But now it seemed…it seemed worse, somehow. Maybe because when she thought of kissing she could still feel Adham's lips moving against hers, still feel the hard press of his chest, the way it had felt to be in his strong arms. As though she were something exquisitely special and fragile. He'd held her firmly enough to keep hold of her, gently enough that she wouldn't break.

It was *him* she wanted to touch again. Not just a random man—even if that man had given her a ring. Hassan still seemed random to her. A stranger. While Adham…she felt as if she was starting to know him. To care about him in spite of his hardened nature. Or maybe because of it.

She wanted to reach him, to find out if there was anything soft behind the hardened wall he placed between himself and the world. She wanted to find the root of his scars—not only those he bore physically, but the ones that ran far beneath the surface of his skin. She wanted to soothe his pain.

She looked at him again. The heat had been extinguished, his eyes now cool, flat and black. Perhaps she was imagining everything. The heat and the softness. Maybe he was all rock. But she didn't really believe that.

"Do you want to walk or drive?" he asked, pulling her coat from the peg and handing it to her, his fingers brushing hers. The sweet, unexpected contact giving her body a jolt.

"Always walk. I love taking in the sights."

The evening air was crisp, and she enjoyed the bite of it on her skin—especially with Adham's solid warmth so close to her. It was easy to pretend that it was a date.

Now, dating she'd dreamed of—and often. She'd shut out thoughts of sex, because in a lot of ways it was too challenging, since she knew she would only ever experience it with one man—a man selected by her family for his status, not for any other reason. But dating...

Just being with a man—the companionship, the romance. She'd thought about that so often late at night. Wondered what sort of man she would pick for herself. What it would be like to hold hands, to have her first kiss.

Well, kissing accomplished—even if it hadn't been anything like she'd imagined—but no hand-holding. That seemed a bit backward. But she was certain Adham wouldn't be looking to remedy it.

She forgot about hand-holding—well, she didn't forget, but she shuffled it to one side—when she saw the cinema.

It was everything she'd imagined, with neon lighting and brightly lit posters that reflected off the pools of rainwater on the sidewalks, adding a dim glow to the darkening streets.

"Wow. It's gorgeous," she said, then felt embarrassed—because it was such a typical thing for most people, yet it was amazing to her in that moment.

"You want to take a picture, don't you?"

"It's only a movie theater, Adham," she said pragmatically, arching her eyebrow.

"Yes, but you still want a photo. Just like you needed to take a picture of your blue door." He said it now as though he understood, and that made her heart ache with a need that frightened her. It was intangible, something she hardly understood, but so raw, so real, she thought she might double over with the intensity of it.

She couldn't speak past the lump in her throat as she pulled her camera from her purse and clicked off a dozen pictures of the posters, the lights, the curve of the architecture. She would always remember how she'd felt as she'd stood and looked at this theater. Every time she saw the photos she would remember. Adham's warmth. His unexpected understanding. The pain in her chest.

She looked at the screen on the camera, at the pictures she'd taken. He positioned himself behind her, studying the photos. His fingers bruised the tender hollow of her neck as he brushed her hair back. "You see beauty in so many places. So many things," he said, his voice husky.

Her heart thundered heavily in her chest. "Sometimes people miss beauty because it's buried in everyday objects. But none of this exploration is everyday to me."

He laughed softly, his breath hot against her cheek. "There is certainly nothing everyday about you."

She turned to face him then, and she caught the barest hint of warmth in his expression before the hardened mask returned and he stepped away, his body tensing.

"We should go in, or we'll miss our showing," he said, moving away from her and opening the door to the theater, allowing her to go in first.

It didn't escape her notice when he paid for her ticket. That made it feel even more like a date. He bought her popcorn too—greasy and over-salted, and one of the best things she'd ever tasted.

She was excited about the film—until the lights went down and she suddenly realized how close and intimate it seemed to be seated next to Adham, so close, in the dark.

She shifted and her arm grazed his. Her heart jumped into her throat. She sneaked a glance at Adham out of the corner of her eye. He sat, rock-solid, his expression betraying nothing, the planes and angles of his face stoic. His features were sharper, more defined in the flickering light of the movie screen, his scars deeper, more exaggerated.

Thinking of someone harming him, of him being forced into a life or death situation, made her feel physically ill. She felt sorry for the woman who loved him. He said he didn't want to get married, but her brother hadn't wanted to get married again, and all it had taken was the right woman. The right woman would find Adham, but *her* life would be a misery of worry. She could picture Adham's wife, curled up in bed alone, wondering if that night was the night her husband would never return.

Isabella's heart lurched into her throat. When the picture in her mind had sharpened, the woman she'd seen sitting in bed in the dark, her knees drawn up to her chest, had been *her*.

She blinked and turned her focus back to the movie, back to the story unfolding in front of them, and for a while she was carried away by the beautiful classic romance.

But when the hero finally kissed the heroine she was reminded of what it had felt like when Adham's lips had moved over hers, his tongue sliding against hers, the friction making her nipples tighten and her breasts ache. Like they were doing right at that moment.

She took a piece of popcorn from the tub and his fingers brushed hers. A short gasp escaped her lips, and she shot him another quick look to make sure he hadn't heard. If he had, he certainly wasn't showing it.

Why did he have to appeal to her so much? Why couldn't her chaperon be short, fat and completely horrible? Why did he have to be this enigma of a man who called to everything feminine inside her?

Adham had opened up a new world of fantasies and desires—made her ache for things she'd never wanted before.

It was pointless and cruel. She didn't even have the hope of a brief romance with him, let alone a happily ever after.

She looked at his hands, curled around the shared armrest that sat between them. She examined those scars again. She doubted a brief, light romance with a man like him would even be possible. He was the sort of man who would give nothing or everything. There wouldn't be much in between. And she…she would only be able to give everything. And she would want everything in return. An impossible situation even without the ring on her finger.

His hand brushed hers again and she nearly jumped out of her skin. Attraction, she was discovering, was about a lot more than butterflies in your stomach. It could be all-consuming, a need as elemental and necessary as food or drink. It was quickly becoming that way for her.

Curiosity. That was all it was. It had to be. After all, she'd never really felt drawn to a man like this before. All of the men she'd met at galas and balls and parties had been…insipid. Especially when she compared them to Adham.

Maybe if she were to meet another man like Adham she would feel the same way. Maybe she simply had a type. Except there wasn't another man to equal him. She was certain of that.

When the credits finally rolled on the movie she let out a gust of breath she hadn't been aware she'd been holding. She needed distance, or she was afraid she might crawl out of her skin.

Adham's swift exhalation of breath shocked her. It was almost as though he'd been experiencing the same thing she had. As if he were held in the thrall of this attraction, just as she was.

Once again realism compelled her to ask why on earth a man of Adham's experience would be interested in a virgin princess who didn't even know proper kissing technique.

"Did you enjoy the movie?" he asked as they exited the theater, his voice clipped, his manner detached.

"Yes. I did." Hopefully he didn't want a summary, because all she would be able to give him was a recap of how many times his arm had accidentally brushed hers.

"I'm glad." He didn't sound glad. He sounded detached. Bored. That irritated her. She felt edgy and… and turned on. And he was *bored*.

She couldn't stand next to him anymore—not feeling as if every nerve ending was on fire, as if the light touch of the breeze was going to tip her over the edge into the dark depths of arousal. Discomfiting to a woman who had scarcely experienced arousal in her life—at least not in such a personal sense.

She walked ahead of him, her steps quick and staccato, her heels clacking loudly on the pavement. He was infuriating. Yes, it would really be pointless for him to feel the same way, because neither of them could act on it, but it would have gone a long way toward satisfying her if she knew that he was at least half as uncomfortable as she was.

He kept pace behind her, obviously unconcerned with her pique, which just made her feel more irritated. No wonder women in romantic movies acted so strange sometimes. Men were infuriating. No two ways about it.

"Isabella." His deep voice startled her, and she wobbled on her high heel, her ankle rolling as she pitched to the side.

A strong hand clamped tightly around her arm and kept her from crashing to the cement. She found herself drawn tightly against his firm, muscled chest, his heart pounding heavily beneath her cheek.

"Be careful," he bit out, still holding her.

"It's the shoes," she said, unable to catch her breath, her hands shaking from the adrenaline surge of her near fall—and from his hold on her arm.

"And the fact that you were stomping off like an indignant teenager."

She drew herself back so that she could look at him, conscious that the action pushed her breasts against him. "I was not acting like an indignant teenager."

"Yes, you were."

"I was not!" She looked at his face, at his maddeningly flat, controlled expression. "Does anything *ever* get to you?"

"No."

"Well, it does to me. It seems like I feel everything and you feel nothing." She had only intended to reference the way she felt about shopping and blue doors, but she knew that it hadn't sounded that way. Knew that she had meant much more than that. She wanted to call the words back as soon as she'd spoken them. She'd all but broadcasted her attraction to him, and he was just staring at her, controlled as always.

"You don't think I feel anything, Isabella?" he said, his voice soft, as tightly reined as the rest of him.

He drew his finger over the line of her jaw, his dark eyes intent on hers, and then she felt it—the first crack in his façade. A slight tremor in his hand, unveiled heat in his eyes. Her heart-rate ratcheted up several beats per minute.

"I feel. Things I have no business feeling. I want things that are not mine to covet."

He moved slightly, drawing her back away from the glaring streetlight and turning her, pressing her against the side of one of the buildings. The chill from the brick seeped through her sweater. But Adham was still holding her, and his heat was more than enough to keep her warm, to make her feel as if she might be incinerated where she stood, reduced to a pile of ash at his feet.

"What do you think I felt watching you flaunt all that sexy lingerie? Watching you tease me?"

She opened her mouth to protest at his words.

"Yes, Isabella, you *were* teasing me."

"Yes," she said, her throat almost too tight to allow the word passage.

"And tonight? Sitting with you in the dark? You think I felt nothing? With your soft body so close to mine? Your sweet scent enticing me?" His tone was rough now, his hold on her tightening.

And her body was responding.

"You…you're always controlled."

"Not always." He pressed into her, the hardness of his erection evident against her thigh. "Not always."

And then he was kissing her, his mouth rough at first, demanding, as it had been the first time they'd kissed. She whimpered, wiggled so that she could put her arms around his neck and hold him closer, angling her head so that she could part her lips and kiss him back.

Then something happened. His hold gentled, his lips softened, and the slide of his tongue against hers slowed, became almost leisurely, as though he were savoring the taste of her. The thought sent a sensual shiver through her body, made her moan and arch against him.

He moved his hands down, sliding over her curves, cupping her breasts. She gasped. No man had ever touched her like this before. And he was almost reverent in his exploration of her, as though she were a masterpiece.

"Oh, yes…" She tilted her head back, her breath broken, her words a half-sob.

He rocked against her, his hardness teasing her, tantalizing her, igniting passions she'd never dreamed imaginable. He moved his mouth away from hers, pressing his lips against her neck, biting her gently and then lapping the sting away with his tongue before taking her mouth again.

"Adham…" she sighed against his lips

He abandoned her mouth, breaking contact with her

abruptly. The sudden rush of air against her body was a
shock to her system. He pushed himself away from her,
using the wall as leverage, his chest rising and falling
sharply, his breath visible in the cool night air.

Embarrassment mingled with unquenched desire,
making her feel nauseous, making her knees weak. Now,
with only the chill of the brick against her back, and none
of Adham's solid warmth, she shivered.

"Adham?" She reached out her hand to touch his forearm, and he jerked back with a harsh intake of breath.

"No."

"But…"

He took her hand then, held it up beneath the street-
lamp until the engagement ring on her finger glittered
in the yellow light. "No."

She snatched her hand back, her head swimming, her
body shaking. She had forgotten for a moment—about
Hassan, about Adham's position working for her fiancé,
about her own position in life. There had only been
Adham. His arms, his lips, the hardness of his body.

But now reality was back with a vengeance.

She was engaged to be married.

But she wanted another man with a ferocity so strong
that it made her feel as though her heart was being torn
in two.

Adham paced the length of his office, his body raging at
him, his blood pounding hard through his system. He was
still hard. He wanted her with a need that defied anything
he had known before, a desire that rocked all the control
he had so carefully built up over the years.

He and Hassan had been thrust into adulthood, into
power, in their early teens. Hassan, the oldest by two
years, had assumed the throne; Adham had taken control

of the military, of national security. Both of them had been required to put away childish things and embrace manhood, embrace control. Sacrifice, duty and honor.

But this…girl…this virginal princess, with the face of an angel and a body that could make a man lose every last shred of sanity, had cracked it—had made him do something he had sworn he would not.

He'd left the little temptress sitting in the living room, her black hair tumbled wildly over her shoulders, her eyes bright with desire and embarrassment. He didn't trust himself to be in the same room with her—didn't trust that he would not press her back into the soft couch, settle between her thighs so that she could feel his hardness against the place he knew ached for him. He wanted to cup those luscious breasts again, then tease her nipples, explore them more thoroughly. He'd felt their aroused peaks against his palms and he longed to see them—the shape of them, the color—to taste them with his tongue, suck them into his mouth…

He swore violently and picked his mobile phone up from the desk, dialing his brother's number. There was no answer. Little wonder. Hassan was a busy man, and difficult to access at times. At the moment Adham knew he was steeped in diplomatic negotiations, and the delicate process of changing and signing new laws. Just another reason Adham was grateful that the ultimate leadership of his country had not passed to him.

He was a man who needed action, needed to physically see and ensure that Hassan and his people were safe from harm. It was why he had been glad of a military position rather than assuming a diplomatic role.

And now action was needed—with or without Hassan's blessing. He could not stay with Isabella any longer. Not with his control so dangerously cracked. Even now it had not returned to him. Even now he longed to take her, fill her, possess her, make her his woman.

The last few days had been hell. She had paraded her sexy little body for him at the department store, had teased him with the thought of her in that brief lingerie.

It had been far too long since he'd had sex. He needed to get rid of his charge and contact one of his ex-mistresses as quickly as possible, so that he could soothe his raging libido.

He opened the office door and saw that Isabella remained where he had left her, knees drawn up to her chest, her dark hair spilling over her shoulders in a shiny curtain. She straightened when he came out of the office, her expression wary, her cheeks flushed.

"We're leaving," he said tightly.

"What? Where?"

"We're going to Umarah. To the palace. To Hassan."

"But…why?"

"Why?" he said roughly. "I shall tell you why, *amira*. Because back on the street I was thirty seconds away from stripping you of your jeans and taking your carefully guarded virginity against a wall." The words were torn from him, his voice raw. "*You* may be able to betray your word to the High Sheikh in such a way, but I will not."

"I…" Her pretty mouth dropped open, her blue eyes wide.

Good. She was shocked—as he had intended. He had been intentionally crude in order to show her who she was dealing with, show her the disparity between them.

"I don't want to leave," she said quietly, those wide eyes filling with tears.

"I do not care what you want," he said coldly, the roaring of his blood making the words harsh. "We are leaving. *Now*."

CHAPTER SIX

ADHAM'S private plane touched down in the Umarahn capital of Maljadeed just before dark. Even with the sun disappearing behind the flat, rock-hewn mountains on the outskirts of the city, it was the hottest weather Isabella could ever remember experiencing.

The limo that was waiting for them at the airport was air-conditioned, providing immediate relief from the thick, stifling air. The road system was clearly new and expensive—a sign of a thriving infrastructure. It wound through the city, which was still alive with movement despite the late hour. The marketplace was bustling with people selling their wares. The smell of street food and spices mingled together. Crumbling buildings were backed by high-rises, supermarkets next to craft stalls, mixing the old world and the new in a way Isabella had never seen before.

It was a strange place, void of anything familiar. And it was to be her home.

It was a frightening thought—and much more real than it ever had been before. She'd known that she was going to marry Hassan, known that Umarah was destined to be her home, since she was ten years old. But facing it now...seeing how different the city was, how different the road systems were, how strange and foreign the marketplace and the clothing on the people milling around…it was difficult to imagine her life here—what it would be like not only to change homes, to be married, but to change cultures, languages.

She swallowed, longing to draw strength from Adham, to lean against him and have him shield her. But she couldn't. He had made it plain that contact between them was impossible, and he was right. She knew he was. She was engaged to Hassan and she had always planned to honor that—had never even contemplated betraying him.

It was because Adham was a known entity in a land of unknowns. That was all. Nothing more. There couldn't be more.

The palace came into view, set in the middle of everything and shrouded partially by a high stone wall. The dim light made the palace glow purple, the domed roof a pale yellow. She imagined that during the fiery heat of the day it was an intense sight.

Her stomach bottomed out, her heart twisting in her chest. She was about to come face to face with the man she was to marry. About to meet the Sheikh who had gifted her with his ring. The man she did not want. While she stood next to the man she'd grown to desire. The man who was slowly winding his way around her heart with his hardened demeanor and his battle scars.

Adham opened her door for her and she got out of the limo, trying to avoid brushing against his hard body. She was too weak for that. She couldn't touch him without betraying how much she wanted him, how much she ached. And she did—her stomach, her heart and her head hurt.

Suddenly the thought of being separated from Adham made her want to sink to her knees and weep, made her want to cling to him in desperation. She had no idea what it meant, only that it seemed like life or death.

She kept her arms tightly at her sides to discourage him from placing his hand on her. If he touched her, even by accident, she would shatter. She noticed he was holding himself rigid too, his jaw tense, his entire body locked tight, his muscles strained as though he were engaged in a physical war.

But that horrible, flat look in his eyes made it impossible to read what he was truly thinking. Only the tension in his body made her aware that there was anything behind the stony mask he wore. She hated it. Hated that she couldn't read him. Hated that what she needed more than anything was comfort. From him. Comfort she was certain he wouldn't—couldn't—give to her.

She gripped her arms, trying to stop her teeth from chattering. Nerves swept over her. She swallowed convulsively, trying to keep from crying. She felt ridiculously weak, and she also felt like her life was ending.

They walked up a long walkway lined with ash trees that were immaculately trimmed, as was the bright green lawn. The greenery was a show of the High Sheikh's wealth, Isabella assumed. Water in a desert nation was likely worth more than gold or oil.

The double doors to the palace were opened by two armed guards who stood still, faces stoic, as she and Adham passed them and walked into the outer chamber.

The palace in Turan was beautiful, but it was comprised of hand carved stone and antique, woven tapestries, sedate next to the inlaid marble that covered the domed walls and ceiling in the entryway of the Umarahn palace. The floors were black high-gloss tile, the walls a deep green and blue, with fine gold filigree separating the different stones. There was so much color—color that was designed to show the riches of its owner.

"So," she said, exhaling, "this is my palace?"

A short laugh escaped Adham's lips. "Indeed it is, *Principessa*." The Italian version of his usual name for her made her heart trip. His accent was more pronounced when he spoke Italian—a language he was obviously less comfortable with than English. She found it very sexy, his heavy Arabic accent putting a unique stamp on her native language.

She turned her face away from him sharply. There was no point in lingering over all the things about Adham she found attractive. Not when she was about to meet her future husband.

She gritted her teeth, fighting the sting of tears again.

A man dressed in flowing robes came sweeping into the room, and Isabella's heart sank. But as he walked closer she could see that it was not her fiancé. She'd only seen a couple pictures of Hassan, but she remembered his face.

"Numair." Adham inclined his head.

"Sheikh Adham," the other man returned.

So she'd been right. He was nobility of some kind, an important man. Not simply a bodyguard.

"I am here to see High Sheikh Hassan. I bring him his bride." Adham's words were clipped, his manner formal.

Numair looked to the side, as though he were reluctant to look at Adham directly. "Hassan is not here. He is on retreat."

Adham stiffened. "And how long will he be gone?"

This time Numair turned shifty eyes to her. "He is to be…delayed until the wedding, I'm afraid."

"I see. Please bring someone to show the Princess to her room."

Relief washed through her. She didn't have to face Hassan. Not today. Not for another two months. But she was still to be confined to the walls of the palace. Would Adham leave her here alone? The idea made her stomach churn with nerves.

"You will not accompany me?" she asked, hating the obvious fear that edged her voice.

"It would not be appropriate," he said tightly, not looking at her, his eyes fixed ahead, his hands locked behind his back. "Hadiya will show you to your chambers."

A small girl with glossy dark hair and a sweet smile came into the room as if on cue. *"Salaam,"* she said, inclining her head, and Isabella returned the greeting.

Isabella followed Hadiya, but she was powerless to stop herself from looking back at Adham. His eyes were fixed on her, intensity blazing from them. She felt the heat burn through her, her stomach contracting sharply. She whipped her head back around and turned her focus to where she was headed, her heart thundering madly.

"These are the women's quarters," Hadiya said. "Men are not allowed." A slight sparkle lit her dark eyes. "Of course they do not always follow the rules."

Would Adham? He was a man who seemed to live to enforce rules, to ensure that honor was upheld. Which probably excluded visits to the women's quarters. She wasn't sure how to handle that. It felt as though he was her lifeline.

Isabella could only offer a weak smile.

"The High Sheikh had this room prepared for you months ago—for after the wedding."

Isabella nearly sighed with relief. She would have her own room. In her own wing of the house. That way, at least, she would have some space from her husband. The word made her stomach clench.

Hadiya opened a massive door and revealed a spacious room draped in swathes of fabric in rich, saturated colors. They hung from the ceiling, and were draped so that they gathered around the bed like an extravagant canopy. There were doors that led out to what looked like a walled garden. So this was her cage. It was gilded nicely. She would say that for it.

"Thank you, Hadiya," she said.

The girl inclined her head. "I'll bring your things in later."

"Thank you," Isabella repeated, somewhat inanely.

When Hadiya left Isabella fought the urge to give in to her grief. Instead she walked across the high-gloss jade floor and went to stand at the window, pulling the heavy blue drapes back. The garden was lovely—an oasis with man-made waterfalls and flowering trees and bushes. There was a carved stone bench in the middle of all of it.

It was clear that real effort had been put into the space, although it hadn't been tailored to her likes and dislikes specifically. It was simply an elaborate space designed to please any woman. And she *did* like it, so it would be childish to find fault with it simply on principle.

She pressed her forehead against the glass, felt the heat from outside, and hoped that it might warm the chill that was spreading through her.

"Isabella."

Adham's husky voice made her pulse jump. She turned and her heart stopped. He was standing there, her bags in his hands.

"I thought men weren't allowed here," she said.

"We aren't." He set her bags down at the foot of the sumptuous bed.

"You're breaking the rules. Doesn't that violate your code of honor?"

"I'll risk it."

"Are you leaving?" she asked.

He nodded curtly, and she hoped that the devastation she felt wasn't evident on her face. "I have other business to deal with."

"Babysitting another princess?"

A small smile curved his lips. "You're the only one."

"Good." And she meant it. She didn't want to think of him with another woman. Although just because he wasn't princess-sitting it didn't mean he wasn't going to find a woman. One of the women he had an *arrangement* with.

"We're installing a new rig in our oil fields. I like to be on site for major events like that."

"You do so much, Adham," she said. "What have *I* done?"

"You've seen the Eiffel Tower. You have a picture."

"Yes." Now it really did feel as if tears were imminent. Her throat was aching with the effort of holding them back. "I don't have a picture of you, though."

"Bella…" he said, the name so soft and sweet on his lips that her body shuddered.

"Just one." She reached for her purse and pulled out her camera, aiming it at him. His facial expression didn't change.

"Didn't anyone teach you that you need to smile for pictures?" she asked.

Then he smiled, and she felt a tear escape as she captured the moment she'd so longed to see. "You should smile more," she said softly, touching the screen, the image of Adham.

"I don't smile?"

She shook her head. "Not enough."

"I used to."

"What happened?"

A shadow passed over his handsome face, his dark eyebrows locking together. "I had to grow up much faster than I should have. That life experience we've talked about. I know you feel you've been overprotected, but trust me, Bella, it is better than seeing what I have seen."

His hand flexed as he lifted his arm, as if he meant to touch her, but then he dropped it, clenching his hand tightly into a fist. "I'll see you again at the wedding."

He turned and left there, alone, feeling as though something inside her had broken.

"Where are you?" When Hassan finally answered his phone, Adham was on the point of losing his temper with his older brother.

"I'm at the summer palace."

Adham tamped down a surge of annoyance. His brother was at their recreational home—a place they had gone as children for vacations. Before they had lost their parents.

"Well, I am here in Maljadeed, with your bride, only to discover that you are not."

"You were supposed to entertain her in France." His brother actually sounded angry—a rarity.

Adham's pulse quickened at the thought of how he might have kept Isabella entertained had they stayed in Paris. She had become too great a temptation. Hassan was the most important person in his life, the last remaining member of his family and his king. Betraying him was unthinkable. Isabella was only a woman, a beautiful woman, but beautiful women were plentiful. He would be able to find another one now, to help take the ravenous edge off his libido.

"She wished to come here." A lie, but in the circumstances he felt it a well-justified one.

"I cannot come back just yet."

"And I cannot stay here, if that is what you have in mind."

"Adham, please stay with her. I would not ask this of you if it were not so important."

"What is so pressing that your bride becomes my responsibility?"

There was a long stretch of silence before Hassan spoke again. "I am with Jamilah."

"Jamilah"

"She is... I am in love with her, Adham. And soon I must marry Isabella. Jamilah will not have me then. She has told me. She will not be my mistress—and, believe me, I have begged her to change her mind. But what can I do? The contract is signed. I need these last moments. I cannot leave her now."

His gut response to his brother's pronouncement was anger. Anger at the thought of Isabella being betrayed, that his brother was willing to be unfaithful to Isabella once he had made vows to her. He shut it off, ignored it. His loyalty lay with Hassan, not Isabella.

"And you intend me to stay here with your fiancée while you toy with your girlfriend?"

"I am not toying with her," Hassan said, his voice rough. "I have only these two months; do not ask me to sacrifice them."

"I would not," Adham said, clipped.

"Then stay with Isabella, so she does not feel abandoned. I cannot imagine she would wish to be left there at the palace with no one but staff to keep her company."

"Of course not."

"You could take her to see some of the city. Show Isabella her new home. I'll bet she would enjoy seeing the oasis at *Adalia*."

She would enjoy it. She would want to take pictures.

"I will owe you for this, Adham," his brother said, his voice pleading.

Adham gritted his teeth, his grip on the phone tightening. "Yes, you will."

"I'll be indebted to you for this. Gladly."

Adham gave his brother a curt farewell and snapped his phone shut. He had thought to escape the hell of unsatisfied longing he'd been living in back in Paris. He had thought that he would be getting away from his future sister-in-law, gaining distance, plus time with another woman, so that when he saw her again on the day she was to become his brother's wife he would feel nothing.

She is only a woman.

There was no reason that she should tempt him. Yes, she was beautiful—sexy beyond belief. But she was nothing more than an innocent virgin. Virgins held no appeal to him. He enjoyed women with experience. Women who excelled in coy flirtation and sexual games. Women who kept their emotions in control at all times, who were as hardened and cynical as he was. Not women with eyes that were unguarded windows to their souls.

Isabella was not meant for a man like him. He would only tarnish her. He could not give her what she deserved, and neither did he want to. She needed someone who could treat her with softness, possibly offer love—which he had no doubt, given a couple of years to forget his woman, Hassan could do.

Adham had lost the ability to love when he'd watched his mother fall to the ground at his feet, her life snuffed out by an assassin's bullet. His father had met with the same end. Only he and Hassan had remained. Adham had been able to keep Hassan barred from the room—had spared him the sight, spared him the injury.

But *he* had seen. He had watched his parents die in front of him. It was only by a twist of fate the bullet he had taken hadn't killed him too.

Years in military service and protecting his country had helped the wounds created on that day to scar over, to harden completely. There had been times when he had been forced to choose between his own life or the life of his enemy. The fact that he lived was testament to the choices he'd made.

He could not offer a woman love. Did not know how to be a husband or a father. His hands—hands that had taken life—could never cradle a child.

Even if Hassan were not in the picture, he would not touch Isabella.

There would be no taking the edge off tonight. Yes, there were women who worked in the palace who would be willing to come to his bed, but he would not take advantage of them in such a way. And, no matter what his plans had been, he would not sleep with one woman while picturing the face of another.

He stalked into the bathroom that connected to his chambers. The only way he would be able to relax tonight would be with the aid of a cold shower.

When Isabella emerged from her room the next morning to find some breakfast, Adham was sitting at the dining table, with nothing but a mug of coffee placed in front of him.

"I thought you would have left." She hoped the surge of happiness that had just rocked her wasn't totally obvious in her tone. It disturbed her, the intensity of the joy that overtook her when she saw that he was still there, when she saw he hadn't abandoned her.

"Hassan is detained, and shall be until the wedding. He has asked that I stay with you so that you are more comfortable." There was no warmth in his voice. It was clear by how he spoke that he didn't want to be with her.

"Did he order you to stay?"

"No. But I would not feel right about leaving you here by yourself."

"I would be fine." Three servants came into the room, one carrying a carafe filled with coffee, one with a platter of fruit, the other with two bowls of some kind of hot grain cereal. "And I would hardly be alone," she said, as one of the bowls was set in front of her.

"Should there be a security issue, I would feel better being here."

"Is that a possibility?"

"It's always a possibility. When Hassan is here it will fall to him to protect you, but as he is not I will ensure that you're safe."

"Thank you," she said stiffly.

She was glad he was staying. In fact she was much happier about it than she should be. And that made her wish he had left. What was the point of nurturing her feelings for him? Feelings that were growing along with her attraction to him, despite her best efforts.

"If you wish to explore I could take you to see *Adalia*. It's an oasis about two hours from here that the royal family has used for centuries. In times of war, or imminent threat, they would escape to the desert and wait until the danger had passed."

The idea of escaping the confines of the palace made her feel as though a band that had been slowly tightening across her chest had loosened, enabling her to breathe again.

"Yes, I would like that."

"You will have to change into suitable clothes. Hadiya can help you with that."

Suddenly she was brimming with excitement again. She wasn't simply going to be locked in the palace until the wedding. She was going to be with Adham.

And, as foolish as it was, she felt that if she was with Adham the most important piece of her life was in place.

CHAPTER SEVEN

ISABELLA could tell they were getting closer to the oasis when the sparse scrub brush that lined the road began to grow taller, the color deepening, giving way to a line of cypress trees that reached to the faded blue sky.

"You were right," she said softly, her eyes trained on the horizon, on the flat topped rocks that looked as though they had been set right on top of the red sand, "it is beautiful."

"And dangerous."

"Life is dangerous, though, isn't it, Adham?"

She noticed his knuckles whiten as he gripped the steering wheel of the off-road vehicle more tightly. "It can be."

"You know that more than most people, don't you?"

"Why do you ask that?"

"Because you're always telling me how much life experience can take from you. I imagine you must have personal experience with that."

"I was in the military," he said, his voice clipped. "You see things…do things that are not always easy. But it was to protect my country and I cannot regret it."

"But you do." She looked out of the window, at the fruit trees that were starting to appear with increasing frequency. "Have you ever been shot?" She didn't really want to hear the answer—didn't want to imagine him in so much pain.

"Yes. I have also had to use my weapon against others." He paused, and the full meaning of his words gripped her, took root. "No matter the reasoning, taking another man's life is not something to find pride in."

She shook her head. "You wouldn't. I know you wouldn't. You would have had to have good reason." She believed it. Absolutely and implicitly. She knew Adham would never harm someone unless it was to save his own life, or the life of an innocent party.

"You know this for sure?"

"You're a good man, Adham. Even when you irritate me I don't doubt that."

"I irritate you?" he asked.

"Sometimes. But I know that I irritate you as well."

"Sometimes," he agreed easily.

She was glad to hear some humor in his voice. Especially after the bleakness she'd heard when he'd spoken of his time in military service.

"Is this man-made?" she asked, staring at the rock crag that seemed to have grown straight out of the desert sands, arcing over them slightly, providing very heavy cover from the midday sun and making shade for trees and animals beneath its bulk.

"No. This is God's provision. Even in the desert there is life, if you know where to look."

They drove around the curved rock and stopped in front of a large pool of water. It was surrounded by rock, a solid stone basin, with plants and palms growing thick and green all around the perimeter. And beyond that, set into the unexpected jungle, was a large tent, barely visible behind the thick fronds of the trees.

"This is certainly a good refuge," Isabella said, opening the car door and stepping out into the warm air. It was dry, and still very hot, but the rocks, water and plant life absorbed some of the heat, making it warm, but not scorching as it was out on the sands.

Adham got out of the vehicle and surveyed their surroundings. He looked as though he was a part of the landscape, as if he belonged. As though he alone could tame this wild beauty.

She was suddenly very aware of how alone they were. They had no servants with them, no chaperons. Because Adham was her chaperon. The High Sheikh's most trusted man.

But he had violated that trust in Paris. He had kissed her. Had wanted her. And she couldn't forget that. Her body wouldn't let her. She wondered if he was as plagued by it as she was, or if she was just one woman he'd desired in a long line of many.

"The tent is designed to house staff and all the members of the royal family in total comfort. There is plenty of privacy available," he said, answering some of the questions that had been rattling around in her head.

He hoisted her bag from the back seat of the Jeep and slung it over his broad shoulder with ease, the muscles in his back shifting beneath his button-up safari-style shirt. She followed him as he moved toward the tent, her footsteps awkward and heavy in the work boots she wore, which came halfway up her shins and made walking stiff.

"Why are we wearing boots?"

"Snakes," he said carelessly.

She sped up then, walking alongside him. "Snakes?"

"It's the desert, *amira*."

"I know that. And I know that there are several species of snake native to the area. I just didn't think you would take me anywhere there might be serious danger from them."

"There isn't serious danger from them, but there is a possibility of running into them. They like to keep cool, and they need water. This is a very attractive place for wildlife."

"Well, it is beautiful." She jumped to the side slightly, after hearing a rattle in the dry brush, but managed not to shriek or do anything horribly embarrassing. "Are there a lot of oases in Umarah?"

"A few. Several along the most common trade routes. But this one has been a well-guarded secret for many generations. So you might run into snakes, but not other people."

"I love that there's a way for even the hottest desert to be habitable. It doesn't seem possible for all this life to be hiding in the middle of the sand…but it is."

He turned and offered a smile. Her heart stuttered, and she wished she had her camera at hand. "I told you that there is beauty for those who are willing to look."

It was there in Adham as well. She knew it. He tried to keep people out—at least he tried to keep *her* out—but she could see there, underneath all the layers of rock, what a good man he was. Strong, but also compassionate—firm, but understanding. He would make a wonderful leader. It was a shame *he* wasn't the ruler of Umarah. A shame he couldn't be the man she was meant to marry.

He doesn't even want to get married.

Still, she was thinking that being Adham's unwanted bride would be better than belonging to a man she didn't love while she longed for another. And how had that happened? She had been determined to be faithful to her fiancé, to be true to their arrangement. She doubted if this raging attraction, combined with the increasingly tender feelings she had for Adham, landed beneath that heading.

The tent was more like a permanent dwelling than the sort of thing she'd been imagining. There were hand-woven rugs on the floor, providing a plush surface for tired feet if the inhabitants had been traveling. Lanterns hung low from the support beams, well away from the canvas that made up the tent.

There were big blocks of canvas hanging from the sides, dividing rooms, creating privacy. The living area was large and open, with divans and plush couches placed around in a wide half-circle, perfect for a big gathering. She could imagine it filled with people, laughter.

"I really love it."

"I'm glad," he said, setting her bag on the floor. "It's a special place for the al bin Sudar family."

"I wonder if Hassan will want to take vacations here," she said idly, running her hands along the rich velvet of a red divan. Even her own father had taken them on vacations. They had homes on the outlying islands near Turan, and in Italy. Those times, away from palace life and some of the protocol, were her very favorite memories.

She and Hassan would have children, if all went according to plan. It would stand to reason that he might want to come here with them someday. The thought caused a stab of pain to pierce her chest.

It didn't seem right, thinking of having Hassan's children. She didn't even know the man…and the only man she could imagine having children with was Adham. Why? When had that happened? Why was her heart so tied to this hard man who showed less emotion than granite at times?

Hassan was a handsome man. She remembered that from his picture. Being married to him wouldn't be a terrible thing. She had never been repulsed by the thought, though it hadn't exactly made her jump for joy either. But now…now it seemed so wrong. Adham was the man she desired, the man she.… *No.* She wouldn't go there. She could not. There was no point in it.

Adham watched Isabella run her fingers lightly over the furniture. His body tightened as he imagined those delicate hands on his body, even as his stomach churned with rage at the thought of her vacationing with Hassan, the thought of her bearing Hassan's children.

It was a betrayal—of his brother, his country—to despise the thoughts and yet he did. He could not abide the thought of another man touching her—even if that man were his brother, a man who, according to the contract signed by Isabella's father and by Hassan, had every right to her.

He had brought her here at Hassan's suggestion, and also to prove to himself that he could master his desire for her. And he could. There was no other option. It didn't matter that she appealed to him more than any woman in his memory. She was to be a member of his family, a part of his existence, a woman he was sworn to protect for the rest of his life. He had to master his body's response to her, not simply sublimate it.

It was simply his denied libido reminding him that it had been six long months since he'd had a woman in his bed. A swim in the cold water later would take care of it. Isabella was much happier here than she'd been at the palace. He'd seen the life leech from her when they'd entered the palace at Maljadeed, but here…it seemed returned to her. It made the trip more than worth it. Even if there was a small amount of torture he would have to endure.

He could understand how she'd felt in the confines of

the walled palace. It was a difficult place for him as well. It was where his family had been killed. It represented the darkest moments of his life. It was one reason he had always been grateful he'd come into the world two years after Hassan. He had no desire to rule, to care for matters of State. To be trapped in the palace where he had lost his family.

He always felt most free in the desert—less shackled to the bonds his position demanded of him, less tied to the things of the past. In the desert his mind had to be in the present. Watching the weather for torrential downpours and sandstorms, keeping an eye out for dangerous wildlife.

He would welcome the respite from Maljadeed.

Adham cleared his throat. "Hassan is not a big fan of being out in the desert. He prefers the luxury provided by our palaces. There are several in different parts of the country. One on the coast. You will enjoy that one. It might remind you of your home."

"It's funny...I find I haven't really missed my home... Turan. I've felt more at home away from my family than I ever have in my life. I think it's because I was finally able to be myself. I was away from everyone's expectations of me." She looked at him then, a small smile tugging her lips. "Well, not everyone's. But you...I've actually enjoyed being with you."

His chest suddenly felt tight.

"Are you hungry?" he asked, knowing it was abrupt, realizing it was the question he always asked when he wanted to divert her.

"Yes." It always worked.

"Hassan ordered some staff members to come here ahead of us and stock the fridge."

"There's a fridge?"

"There are windmills nearby, and they provide a small amount of power. That way, if there's a need to charge a satellite phone, or if we need to keep food cold, it's available. For lights we still use the lanterns."

"Very efficient."

"We believe in using the resources the desert provides us with." A movement Adham had spearheaded. He'd begun drilling in the middle of the uninhabitable places in the desert, had started programs that employed harnessing solar and wind power to provide the people with electricity even in remote places.

"I like that. You'll have to talk to my brother about all of this. He'll be very interested in bringing this kind of thinking to Turan."

Adham moved through the room to the small refrigerator that was in the corner. He pulled out a platter with fresh fruit, stuffed dates and meats and cheeses. His gut clenched. His brother had planned his fiancée's seduction for him. He could not have given him better tools—unless there was also champagne in an ice bucket somewhere. Which, given his surroundings, he would not discount.

"Lovely!" Isabella said, her eyes bright.

Seeing all that excitement on her beautiful face, an excitement that seemed to be aroused by things he hardly noticed, caused a strange tightness in his entire being. She seemed to revel in everything—the taste of foods he took for granted, views he had seen thousands of times. They were all things that brightened her face, things that brought about her unbridled joy.

He lived his life with his emotions kept carefully in check, yet Isabella wore hers boldly. She had said back in Paris, just before he had made the mistake of kissing her, that she felt everything. It seemed that she did.

She sat on the divan, her legs tucked under her, eyes

bright with happiness, her dark hair tumbled over her shoulders. The sight made him ache. Blood pulsed, hot and hard, down to his groin. He wanted her. *Her.* Not a nameless, faceless woman to take the edge off his desire.

He wanted Isabella Rossi—his brother's fiancée. But that was a line he refused to cross. He would not abandon everything of importance in his life to find physical satisfaction in the arms of a woman. Even if it was a woman who called to him, body and soul, more than anyone ever had.

Isabella couldn't sleep. It was comfortable in the tent; the night air of the desert was cool. She could hear thick drops of rain hitting the canvas roof, beating on it mercilessly. She knew that sudden downpours, along with flash flooding, were common in this region. But it wasn't fear that kept her awake.

No. She was so hot inside. Burning. Emotions were at war with desire—a desire that was growing quickly into a need as powerful as her need for food. Water. Breath.

She didn't know what it was she felt for Adham. She wasn't certain she wanted to know. It was nothing she had planned. She'd wanted to get to know herself better. To find out if she liked blue because she liked it, or because her mother had told her it flattered her coloring. She'd found a lot more than that, and with it she'd started a battle inside herself.

She swung her legs over the side of the bed and stood, padding out into the living area. Adham was there, reclining on a divan, his eyes closed, his muscles tensed, sleep obviously eluding him.

"You can't sleep either?" She pulled her robe tightly around herself. Beneath the robe she was wearing the peach negligee, but she felt reasonably secure with thick terrycloth covering her curves.

"I don't sleep very often." He opened his eyes and straightened.

She noticed his jaw tighten, noticed the muscles in his forearms tensing as he looked at her. A rush of feminine satisfaction rocked her. Never had she felt more beautiful than in that moment—barefoot, in a robe, and making Adham very uncomfortable.

"It's hard for you to rest and it's hard for you to smile," she said, feeling sad for him. He really was an example of life experience being a bad thing. She wished she could shield him from it. Offer him some comfort. She wished it with everything she had.

The ring on her left hand suddenly felt very heavy. Because it was holding her back, keeping her from what she desired most. She had thought it was freedom that she wanted, but freedom seemed like an empty, elusive thing now. Something that didn't matter—not if she had it alone, not if she didn't have Adham.

"But everything else is so easy for me," he said, dark humor lacing his voice.

"That is true. I won't challenge you there." She pulled a downy blanket from one of the sofas and sat on the soft floor, wrapping the blanket around her shoulders. "Duty and honor—that seems to come easily to you. You *want* to do it. I…I'm just sort of going along with it. It seems meaningless. But you…it means something to you."

"Because I have seen what happens when men turn from it. If I do not protect the High Sheikh, who will? If I do not put my all into protecting my people, where does that leave them? I cannot turn away from it. I cannot resent it."

"I resent my lot in life plenty." She dipped her head

forward and her hair slid over her face, making a shield between Adham and herself.

Suddenly she felt warmth. Adham's warmth. He was kneeling on the floor, his knee nearly touching hers. He brushed her hair back over her shoulder. "Your duty costs you. I understand why you felt the need to escape it. Even for a while."

"You didn't think that at first. What changed your mind?"

"Knowing you. Knowing that you are not a spoiled child, but a woman who simply wishes to make her own decisions."

Tears formed in her eyes, thick and hot, and as she blinked they fell, sliding down her cheeks. Adham brushed them away, his thumbs rough, comforting against her skin.

"Your duty has cost you too," she said, looking at the scars that marred his perfect skin, at the slashing line that started at his collar and disappeared beneath his shirt.

"These scars are nothing," he said, shrugging. "I live. My family does not."

"Your *family*?" Horror stole through her, chilling her, making her shiver.

"My mother, my father…they were killed in front of me. I could not stop it from happening."

"Adham.…" His name escaped her lips on a sigh of anguish. She ached to hold him, but she was certain he wouldn't allow it, so she kept still, kept her hands in her lap.

"That was when I got this." He pulled the collar of his shirt to the side, exposed a light-colored patch of skin that was raised up from his undamaged skin. "I was shot as well. They thought I was dead. That is the only reason I'm alive today. That is why I welcome my duty. I will protect my people, my High Sheikh, from men like that. Men who would kill for money, power, land. Men who would take life for things that mean nothing."

She let her fingertips brush the scar, whispered a prayer of thanks that he was still here, still living, even when his parents were not. Unbidden, her fingers moved to the first button of his shirt, and she pushed the button through the hole, revealing a wider wedge of bronzed skin, revealing more livid scars that marred the landscape of his perfect body.

Without pausing to think she reached out and touched the raised skin. She felt him tense beneath her fingertips, felt his body go rigid with tension. She began to release each button, all the way down, exposing a slim strip of flesh from his chest all the way down to his washboard-flat belly, bared for her inspection. She swallowed, her mouth dry, her heart hammering in her chest, another tear sliding down her cheek.

She moved the edges of his shirt aside, baring a ridge of scars that ran along his ribcage. With the tip of her finger she traced a slashing line that rose up from the waistband of his trousers and extended up through the indentation of his navel. The scars were lighter, ridges of flesh that were hard and smooth.

The body surrounding the damaged skin was perfect. Deep bronze and well muscled, without an ounce of spare flesh to hide his superb definition from her hungry gaze. His chest was sprinkled with just the right amount of dark hair. She let her fingers drift over his muscles, let them slide over the hard-cut edges, the rough hair tickling her fingertips, teasing her senses.

He inhaled deeply, his chest expanding under her hands as she continued to touch him, explore him.

Adham stiffened, pulling away from her hot touch.

His heart was hammering in his chest, his muscles so tight they ached. His whole body ached for her—for her to flatten her palm against his skin, to continue her exploration into more intimate territory. He should stop her. Should have stopped her the moment she placed her hand on him. Yet he had been held—a captive of what she was doing to him, of what she made him feel.

It had started out as an innocent, comforting gesture. Because Isabella *was* an innocent. A virgin. A woman he had no business touching.

Some of the fractured light from the overhead lanterns danced over her hand, made the ring on her finger glitter brightly. He gripped her wrist and pushed her away.

"Bella," he said roughly, "do you know what you're doing to me?"

She moved closer to him, her eyes glistening with hurt and a heartbreaking undertone of confusion. "I hope it's close to what you're doing to me. I hope I'm not the only one that feels this."

She licked her lips and leaned in, pressing a kiss to the first scar. His muscle, his body, jumped beneath her lips. She slid her hand up to his pectoral.

"I've never touched a man like this before," she said softly.

Arousal pounded through him. Unneeded. Unwanted. And hotter than anything he'd ever experienced before in all his thirty-one years. That an innocent could appeal to him like this—could tempt him to betray the man he protected above all others, the brother he had always loved more than his own life, made him feel as though he were bewitched. He wanted to break the spell, and yet he was caught in its thrall. And part of him was so unbelievably tempted to see what would happen if he gave in.

If a simple touch could arouse him so easily, so intensely, what would happen when he eased inside her slick, tight body? If he made her his.

His.

His heart pounded heavily, his blood flowing hot, thick.

"That night in the alley...I'd never been kissed before that."

She began to move her hand over his chest again, heading to his stomach, and a shock of desire so strong, so overpowering that it nearly undid him, shot through him. He captured her wrist again and pushed her away with more force than he'd intended. She wobbled in her spot on the floor, but caught herself with her hand, her eyes huge, the pain in them clear.

"Bella." Remorse filled him. "Are you hurt?"

"I...no." She shook her head.

He inhaled deeply, trying to clear his head. But he only succeeded in filling himself with her essence. "You must not touch me like that," he said roughly. "Ever."

"Adham, I...I want you so much," she choked. "I want you so much I hurt with it."

He closed his eyes, tried to block out the vision of perfect temptation that she created, with her black hair loose and wild, her full lips reddened with arousal, her cheeks flushed.

A tear slipped down her cheek and he was powerless to stay where he was—powerless to deny the need to comfort her. He drew her to him, wrapped his arms around her, inhaling her scent—uniquely Isabella, and more affecting than any form of torture he'd yet been subjected to.

He slid his hand over the silky black curls, giving himself permission to touch her, if only for a moment. For just one moment he would forget. Forget that this burning ache was forbidden, that she was meant for someone else.

She wrapped her arms around his neck, her moist lips brushing his neck. He closed his eyes, tried to fight against the rising tide of desire that was threatening to overtake him.

"Adham." She lifted her head, her blue eyes intent on his. She leaned in and pressed her lips lightly to his— only for a moment, her movements shy, her inexperience evident.

He held himself still, kept his fists clenched. Because if he allowed himself any sort of free rein he would tunnel his fingers through her hair and devour her mouth, as he had longed to do since the first moment he'd seen her.

She pulled back, the hurt in her eyes almost too much for him to bear. "Don't you want me? I thought…I thought you did."

He ground his teeth tightly together, trying to fight the urge to pull her to him, to take what she was offering. Everything she was offering and more. His heart was pounding, sweat beading on his forehead. He swallowed thickly, the motion almost painful to his hypersensitive body. Everything in him ached for her. And he couldn't take her. *He couldn't.*

She was looking at him, those expressive blue eyes trained on him, wanting answers he shouldn't give.

"I do want you," he bit out, the words torn from him. "But wanting is not the same as taking."

His pulse pounded. His muscles ached. It was taking every ounce of his strength, every bit of his physical and mental willpower, to keep himself from leaning in and tasting her lips. But his control was slipping, the pain of resistance so acute he wasn't certain if he could hold on any longer.

She looked down. "You said…you said I'm an independent woman who makes her own decisions. I've decided that I want you."

Sweet, innocent Isabella, with the words of a temptress rolling off her lips, but without any of the practiced ease he was used to hearing from a woman, undid him completely. The fire that had been burning hot in his stomach exploded into an inferno, igniting his veins, taking over everything.

Life asked too much of him. He had never resented it before. Had never longed to escape his duty until this very moment. But faced with Isabella—beautiful, hungry for him, and with a need that also burned in him like a flame—he wished that he could be a different man.

Then she moved her hands. Her soft palms slid up his chest, over the place where his heart raged inside him. She kissed his jaw. He closed his eyes, everything, every thought, deserting him. There was nothing but this. Nothing but her. Nothing but the need to make her his, wholly and completely, in the most primitive way possible. His body shook with the force of his need, his mind blank of everything. Everything except for her.

Isabella gasped as Adham tightened his hold on her, pulling her onto his lap, bringing her into contact with the hardened length of his erection—the evidence she needed to know that he desired her as she desired him.

Excitement, fear and need slammed into her. Her entire body was shaking with it. Then he leaned in, taking her mouth with a ferocity she hadn't expected, his lips firm, insistent, his tongue hot as it slid between her lips. She moaned, all the fear deserting her. This was *Adham*. The man she desired above all else.

She could have lived her entire life without having her picture taken in front of the Eiffel Tower. She would have been fine if she'd never been to a cinema. But this…she could not have lived never knowing what it was to make love with Adham.

She pushed his shirt from his shoulders, letting it fall to the floor. The sight of him in the flickering lantern light was enough to push her arousal to unbearable heights. She moved her hands over his shoulders, across his back, loving the play of muscles beneath her fingertips, the smoothness of his skin, the heat that radiated from him.

And then she was on her back, his movement so quick and practiced that she hardly realized what was happening until she was flat out, looking at the swags of canvas and the spangled light from the punched-tin lanterns that were lit overhead.

He kissed her jaw, her neck, her collarbone, and she arched into him, running her fingers through his thick dark hair, holding him to her so that he would never stop giving her body attention with that amazing mouth.

His hands were quick at the belt of her robe, loosening the knot and parting the edges slowly, revealing most of her body, barely concealed in the filmy peach negligee. She wasn't embarrassed for him to see her, for her body to be bare to him. She was thrilled beyond words. So excited to have him touching her, to be touching him. She wanted him so much. Beyond reason, beyond anything rational or sane or right. If she could just have him—just once. If he could be the man to show her what it really meant for a man and a woman to be joined… It wouldn't be a lifetime, but maybe…maybe it could be enough.

"I thought of you in this," he said, his voice rough, strained. "And I thought of you out of it." The way he looked at her, the tone of his voice, spoke of how much he desired her. The fact that his need seemed to match hers awed her completely.

He pushed the robe from her shoulders, then slid one of the tiny straps down. His eyes, so dark they were coal-black in the dim light, roamed over her, his breath harsh, fast and shallow.

He put his hand on her breast and moved his thumb over her nipple. It tightened for him, caused exquisite pleasure to shoot through her veins, made the dull ache at the apex of her thighs increase until it was a hollow pain.

She hooked her leg over his calf, pulled him against her, rubbed herself against the thick ridge of his arousal, evident through his jeans, in an attempt to assuage her need.

He tugged the top of the negligee down all the way, revealing her breasts, revealing her nipples, tight with need for him. He groaned and lowered his head, pressed his face to the valley between her breasts, inhaled deeply, slowly. Something about it seemed reverent, as though he were memorizing the moment, her scent, *her.* It made fresh tears spring to her eyes.

Then he rasped his tongue over one tightened bud before sucking it gently into his mouth. His body shuddered and hers matched him, shaking beneath the sensual assault. She dug her fingernails into his back, almost unable to handle the intensity of the pleasure that was rioting through her system.

He turned his attention to her other breast, nipping, licking, sucking until she was trembling beneath him, her body poised on the brink of something monumental, the tension in her belly so tight it had to unravel or she feared she might break.

"Adham," she said, her voice shaky. "Please."

It was all he needed. He stripped his jeans off, kicking them to the side, then pushed her negligee up and pulled the sheer matching panties down in one swift motion.

He touched her, sliding his finger through her slick folds, slipping it inside her. She let her legs fall apart, opened to him, trying to ease some of the tightness she felt. He added a second finger, slowly, gently stretching her, preparing her for him.

Then he moved, replacing his fingers with the blunt head of his erection, pressing his mouth against hers as he eased into her tight body. She gripped his shoulders, digging her nails into his back as she held back a cry of pain. He was big—bigger than she'd expected—and she hadn't realized that it would hurt.

It made her even gladder that it was Adham. How could she trust this moment to anyone else?

She wrapped her legs around his, making more room between her thighs, helping some of the discomfort abate. And then the pain was gone, and waves of pleasure were slowly returning as her body adjusted to his, expanded to accommodate him. It seemed as though she were made for him, and he for her—as though he fit her perfectly, as though they would never be separate again.

And when he began to move inside her the star shapes cast by the lantern light seemed to rain down on her, brilliant flashes of light swirling around her. She felt that tension rising in her again—so tight she could barely move, think or breathe. Then she shattered, as Adham did, her muscles contracting around him as he spilled himself inside her, his muscles quivering, a harsh groan escaping his lips, mingling with her cry of completion.

They lay together, joined still, their breath, harsh and

uneven, the only sound other than the rain that was still pounding against the canvas.

Adham rolled to one side, his arm over his face, his body tense. She reached out and touched his forearm and he flinched, moved away from her. "Get dressed, Bella."

She sat up, tugged her negligee and robe back into place, her heart thundering, her hands shaking. She ached between her thighs, both from pleasure and pain.

"Adham…"

"We are leaving." He stood, taking his jeans from the floor and tugging them on, his movements quick and precise, his face flat, his jaw clenched tight.

She didn't have to ask why. All she had to do was look at her left hand, at the diamond that rested there. The ring that had been given to her by Hassan—by the man he was sworn to protect. She felt sick.

You said I was an independent woman.

Her own selfishness was staggering. She had asked him, pleaded with him to ignore everything that was important to him. But the consequences of this, no matter what they were for her, would be so much worse for Adham.

She loved Adham. She knew that now—understood what had been growing in her from the first moment she'd seen him. Her love for him had made the price worth it to her. But she knew, looking at him now, that it had not been worth it for him. She had been a part of causing him to violate the very core of who he was. There was no love in that. What she had done had been an act of selfishness. And she didn't know if he could ever forgive her for it. She didn't know if she could forgive herself.

CHAPTER EIGHT

ADHAM ignored the pounding rain that was battering the windshield of the military helicopter he was maneuvering through the night sky. Staying at *Adalia* with her was not an option. He had already proven he could not trust himself with her, and he would not prolong a test of his strength that he was destined to fail.

The betrayal that he had committed burned in him—along with an intense, churning arousal that refused to be satisfied.

Half of him was crippled by shame, while the other half was replaying those heady moments of being inside Isabella over and over again. Reliving the tightness of her body, the unquestionable evidence that he was the only man to have joined himself to her, the rush of his orgasm as he'd spilled inside her. It had been heaven. And for that small glimpse of it he had earned himself the hottest spot in hell.

He had shamed himself, betrayed his only family. All for his own pleasure. There was no redeeming his actions.

Yes, Isabella had tempted him, enticed him, but he had acted of his own free will. He alone was responsible for what had transpired between them. His weakness had been the cause.

And now it could not be undone. Her innocence was lost. Innocence he was certain his brother was entitled to per the contract he had signed. Innocence that any traditional Umarahn man would expect of his bride on their wedding night.

Adham had never touched a virgin. And now he had not only taken a woman's virginity, when he hadn't the ability or the intention of offering her marriage, but he had taken the virginity of his brother's woman. His brother's future bride. A greater sin to have added to his already lengthy list he could not think of.

"I won't tell him it was you." Isabella's soft, choked voice brought him out of his thoughts. "I'll let him think it was some boy when I was at boarding school—or a man I met at a ball or something. I won't ever tell him that you were the one I was…with…the first time. Because he'll know, won't he?"

She sounded sick. As sick as he felt at the thought of his brother, of any man, putting his hands on her, joining his body to hers. Everything elemental in him rejected the idea. His body was convinced that Isabella was his, even if his mind knew it was not possible. Even if Hassan's ring hadn't rested on her finger it would be an impossibility.

He was not the man for a woman who saw beauty, excitement in everything. What could he offer her but darkness? His memories of watching his parents die before his eyes? He had seen how painful just hearing him speak of it had been for her. And now her bright world view would forever be tainted with a black spot. Because of *him*.

"Yes. He will know. There was no mistaking it."

She lowered her head, her cheeks turning a deep rose

visible thanks to the bright lights on the dash. "Oh. Was it…did you find it…distasteful?"

Lust and regret swamped him in equal measure, his body burning with both. "There is no good answer to that question, Isabella."

"Maybe not."

He maneuvered the helicopter through the night sky, bringing it in for a smooth landing despite the raging storm.

Isabella finally loosened her grip on the handle above the door, her heart still pounding hard—from nerves and from her proximity with Adham.

He had acted totally unaffected by the weather, and by her—which was much more than she'd been able to manage on both counts. Her entire being still ached with need for Adham. Sex with him had been like a sudden immersion into a new world. She had been so innocent, so much more out of touch with the reality of lovemaking than she'd imagined herself to be. And now she felt as if a veil had been torn from her eyes—as though she could see things clearly, feel things more fully than she ever had before. Unfortunately that included the intense pain that invaded her chest whenever she thought of the reality she now found herself in.

She was promised to another man. And she loved Adham more than she could stand. He had just shown her what it was like to be loved by a man, even if it had only been physical love. And now she had to give it up. Give herself to another man. Even if she didn't she still couldn't have Adham, because he wouldn't want her. And her people, her family, would suffer greatly if she did not honor the contract.

It was her duty. A duty she should have cared for more before she'd compromised everything the way she had.

A tear rolled down her cheek and she wiped it away absently. She would marry Hassan. She would do the one thing that would redeem her in Adham's eyes, even if it meant he would be lost to her forever.

"Do you intend for me to meet with Hassan tonight?"

"I intend to drag him out of bed if I have to," Adham said, his voice cold, uncompromising. A match for his manner.

All the warmth and any semblance of a relationship they had built over the course of the past week together meant nothing to him anymore. And why should it? He was disgusted. With her. With himself. She could read it in him clearly.

She sat in her seat until Adham got out and came around to her side, wrenching the door open and offering her his hand. She looked at it, unable to bring herself to touch him.

"Bella," he said roughly.

She took his hand and allowed him to help her from the helicopter. Water splashed up her legs when she made contact with the wet cement of the helipad.

His hand was warm and firm on hers, his touch almost more temptation that she could bear. The strong flare of desire momentarily immobilized her, rooting her to the middle of the puddle she was ankle-deep in.

His eyes blazed, his chest rose and fell sharply, and the glow from the windows of the summer palace played with the shadows, highlighting Adham's features, his muscular frame and his angular jaw. Her heart hammered hard in her chest. She knew that look—knew it and responded to it. Her blood flowed hotter, faster, her nipples tightened. Her body was readying itself for Adham, for his possession.

"Come," he said sharply, turning and heading down the exterior stairs that led to the heavily guarded second-floor entrance to the massive palace.

It had a more modern look than the palace at Maljadeed—the hallways less cavernous, the displays of wealth much less obvious. Despite the size, it had a look of home, rather than a look of grandeur.

There was a sitting room rather than a formal throne room, and Adham ushered her inside quickly, gesturing for her to sit on one of the divans that lined the wall. A servant girl came rushing in, her expression flustered.

Adham cut off whatever she was about to say. "Go and get to the High Sheikh, tell him I will not be put off."

Isabella's heart was hammering so hard she was certain it was audible. She had told Adham that she wouldn't reveal it was he who had taken her innocence, but she had no idea of what he planned on saying to Hassan when the time came. He might intend to confess her sins for her.

Would Hassan break the agreement? Would he want her imprisoned or exiled? It shamed her now to admit that, while she knew a great many facts about Umarah, she didn't know as much as she should about that aspect of society. One thing she knew for certain was that if Adham's sense of honor was born of Umarahn beliefs, then that wouldn't be an issue. So that concern was eased.

Her heart pounded harder, desperation pouring through her, her palms slick with sweat. "Adham..." She whispered his name. She knew that this was it. She would never touch him again. He was no longer her ally in any way.

But he never had been. Not really. She had fooled herself, and she had done a world-class job.

Then, so lightly she might have imagined it, he swept

his finger along her jaw. One last touch. Barely there. But a connection she needed more than she needed her next intake of air.

"Adham? Has something happened?"

The deep voice entered the room before the man, but when the man followed she knew exactly who he was. His regal bearing gave him away immediately, and then there was his face, which she recognized from his picture. But as he got closer, as she observed the way his long strides carried him over the high-gloss floor, her heart caught. He looked so much like Adham—not precisely in features, but in manner—that she could hardly believe it.

"Everything is fine," Adham responded, his voice even, not a hint of emotion evident.

Hassan's eyes widened when he saw her, his body tensing. *"Principessa,"* he said, his Italian even less polished than Adham's.

She inclined her head, her throat tightening, words deserting her.

"Adham, I need to speak with you in private."

Hassan's words echoed the refrain playing in her own mind. *She* wanted to talk to Adham without anyone else in the room, to ask him who he really was. To ask him why he looked so much like her fiancé that they *had* to be related by blood.

Adham shifted, trying to calm the rush of adrenaline that was still racing through him. He turned and looked at Isabella. Her eyes were narrowed, glittering. She was naive, that was true, but she was smart, and she hadn't missed the fact that Hassan so closely resembled him. In a picture it would be easy to miss, but when they were together it was impossible for anyone to ignore the way their mannerisms were so closely matched. The way they stood, the way they walked, the inflection in their voices. It had been pointed out on many occasions how alike they were.

One of Hassan's servants came into the room as if summoned, which Adham had a feeling she had been. His brother, no matter how careless he might seem at times, never did anything without a plan.

Adham put his hand on Isabella's back. Her heat seared him even as she jumped beneath his touch, but he kept his outward appearance neutral. "Isabella, go to your room and wait there."

He could tell she wanted to argue, but instead she swallowed hard, nodded once, and followed the young girl out. He noticed how stiffly Isabella held her shoulders. He was powerless to ignore the sway of her hips, the way her waist dented in, so narrow, and then gave way to the curve of her round, lush bottom.

"You are familiar with her," Hassan commented, when the doors had closed behind Isabella, blocking her from his view.

Adham swallowed. "I have been with her for over a week—at your bidding, I might add."

"You do no one's bidding but your own, Adham."

It was said goodnaturedly, as a joke. And Adham would have taken it as such even yesterday. But now he could only agree. He had betrayed his brother, and while part of him wanted to confess it, another part of him wished to protect Isabella from the cost of such an admission. Yes, Hassan might know that she was not a virgin after they married, but Adham did not want to expose her.

And, in brutal honesty, he did not want to expose his own lack of control. What had happened with Isabella had been beyond anything in his experience. The way need, desire, lust, had melded together and taken hold of him, gripped him so tightly that he had nearly choked with it, had been completely outside of anything in his reality. He had always considered himself a man with supreme control. He'd always had to be. But Isabella had stripped him of it, unmanned him, and yet at the same time made him feel more of a man, more of a conqueror than he had ever felt he was on any battlefield.

But, as in war, the end result was total devastation.

"I am sorry about your situation with Jamilah, but I cannot be your babysitter any longer. You need to accept responsibility—reality." His chest tightened, as though the words were meant for himself. "Isabella is your fiancée. She deserves to be treated with some level of respect. That means no more running around with your mistress while you use me to keep her busy."

Hassan rubbed his hand over his forehead, suddenly looking much older than he was. Adham had never seen his brother look so torn, so broken. And they had been through the death of their parents together.

A long silence filled the room. Hassan's eyes fixed on the wall behind Adham. Finally he spoke.

"I can't do it, Adham. I know you think I am weak. You have always faced your duty—even when it took you into the middle of a war zone. You have protected our people, sacrificed so much of yourself, while I cannot bring myself to marry the woman who has been given to me. Compared to you, I *am* weak. But I want Jamilah. I *need* her."

Anger shot through Adham—instant and powerful. "It is not a matter of what you want, but what must be done. The alliance with Turan is a necessity. Our people need it. Their people need it. We need the loyalty of their military, an ease in trading, the increase in jobs it will provide. And you would cast that aside?" Even as he spoke Adham knew he was a hypocrite—knew that if anyone had compromised the future of their countries it was him. That if, of the two of them, one was weak, he was the one. And yet that knowledge only fanned the flame of his rage.

"What else am I to do, Adham? Sacrifice myself, Jamilah...our child?" On the last word Hassan's voice cracked. "All for duty and honor? It would make me the better man to many, but it would make me a villain to those who matter most."

"She's pregnant?" As Adham spoke the words he realized it was possible that he had made Isabella pregnant. He hadn't thought of protecting her. He had thought of nothing. He had simply embraced the need that had been pounding through him. He hadn't thought of the consequences, and that included conceiving a child. It seemed a stunning reality when faced with Hassan's inadvertent admission.

"Yes. Would you have me abandon my son or daughter? Should I allow them to become the royal bastard, hiding in hallways, living with the servants, a part of nothing and ridiculed quietly by everyone?"

Adham could suddenly easily imagine Isabella being pregnant. The child being his. He had never wanted children, still didn't, and yet he knew he would never be able to deny that child his birthright. He would never be able to let another man raise that child in his place either.

He tried to force himself to consider his brother's problems and not his own. "Then what do you propose, Hassan?"

Hassan looked away again. "I would not ask this of you, Adham, if it were only for me."

Everything in Adham's body tensed. Always the possibility of his assuming the throne had existed, yet he had never truly imagined it coming to pass. Had never wanted it. He craved action. The physical act of protecting his country. Not signing documents and crafting laws. When he saw a need—like the need for more oil rigs in the desert—he brought it to Hassan, who worked out the finer points of it while Adham set to work on making it a reality in the physical sense.

He disliked the idea of being a figurehead. Hassan was more than that, was a man gifted at creating relationships with world leaders and bringing people around to his way of thinking, but Adham had never envied him the job.

And a part of him—the selfish part, the part that had been in command tonight when he had made love to Isabella—rebelled. Had he not given enough? How much more blood did he have to spill on the sand for the sake of his country? How much more could be taken from him? He didn't want to rule. He didn't want that sort of... confinement. But if not him, who else? There was truly no other choice.

"You want to abdicate." Not a question, for he already knew what his brother intended.

"I don't want to. I find myself in an impossible situation, and I...I feel it is what I have to do."

"What of Isabella?" Adham asked.

"You will marry her," he said, as though it were that simple. As though she could be simply handed from one man to another. "The contract will not be violated, and the alliance between our countries will go forward."

And Isabella would be his.

For a moment he allowed his body to revel in that victory. But then he let his mind take over. Yes, physically he desired Isabella, but he did not wish to marry her. As miserable as she thought she would be with Hassan, she would be even more so with him. He had nothing to offer her. Hassan, at least, would have grown to love her in time. Adham had lost the ability for such fine emotions.

His heart was too scarred.

As he'd watched the life drain from his mother he had vowed he would not let men like those who had killed his parents, men with a lust for money and power—commit such an act on Umarahn soil again, and he had set about making sure it was so. Personally, ruthlessly, until every last one of the dissident factions had been rooted out and destroyed.

The price for that had been his soul, in many ways, and yet he would not have changed it. But it left nothing for a wife—especially for a woman like Isabella.

"I am not suited to her," he said roughly.

"You do not desire her? She's a beautiful woman."

"Yes," Adham bit out. "She is a beautiful woman. Desire is not the issue."

"But you have no desire to marry?" Hassan said, his voice quiet.

No. He didn't want to marry—more for the sake of whoever his bride might be than for himself. He didn't want to rule. But it didn't matter. What he wanted, what he desired, had never mattered.

"What I want is not the issue. You are right. You cannot marry another woman when Jamilah is carrying your child. You are too good a man to let your son or daughter go without recognition. But the contract cannot be broken. You do what must be done, brother, and I will see that everything else is taken care of. I will assume your position as High Sheikh. I will marry Isabella."

Isabella had been putting her personal items away ever since they had been brought to her by one of Hassan's young servants. She had waved off the girl's request to let her see to it. Isabella needed to stay busy—needed to keep her hands occupied.

Adham hadn't told her he was related to Hassan, but she saw it clearly now. That meant she would see him often during her marriage to Hassan.

Hassan. He was a handsome man, but she felt no fire when she saw him. He did not move her. He seemed like a good man—a man who would smile easily, a man who could sleep at night without all of his demons haunting him. But he did not call to her heart. How much easier life would be if he did.

How she felt about him didn't matter, though. What mattered was honoring the contract, doing the best thing for her people, for Adham's people. She had already made a mess of things, but she would not compound her sins by turning her back on her duty.

The door to her bedroom opened. Horror stole over her as she turned, half expecting to find Hassan standing there, wanting to stake some sort of claim on his fiancée. There was no way she could do that. No way she could be with him like that now.

Of course she would have to be with him in that way someday. But not now. *Oh, not now.* Not when Adham's touch still burned on her skin. In her body.

But it wasn't Hassan. It was Adham, his body still, backlit in the doorway, his broad frame highlighted to perfection. Her stomach tightened with need, desire, want, regret—all swirling together, making her dizzy.

When he walked into the room, his face hard, immovable like stone, a chill emanating from him, she felt her heart drop. He was a stranger now, this man who had touched her, taught her what it was to be a woman. The man she loved. In his place was a man guarded by stone—a man even more unknowable than the Adham she had first seen standing at her hotel room door, all hell and fire and determined to bring her back to Umarah if he had to do it by force.

"What are you doing here?" she asked, gripping her elbows, trying to keep from shivering, to keep herself from betraying just how much he did to her by merely walking into a room.

"Hassan and I have spoken."

She noticed his use of the High Sheikh's first name, not his title. "What did you speak to him about?" Part of her hoped he'd confessed their sins, while another part of her had no idea what to want. What had happened between her and Adham had changed her forever, and yet in the real world it changed nothing. She still had to marry Hassan.

In a strange way her journey of self-discovery was responsible for cementing that in her. Being an adult, being her own person, meant nothing if she didn't do all she could for her people. Yes, she had been born into royalty—no choice about it—but, like Adham, she was determined to fulfill her purpose, to serve where she was required to serve. She had great power, great influence, and if she didn't do all that she could with it, it served no purpose.

"Hassan does not wish to marry you."

Her thoughts stalled completely, her brain refusing to function. "I… He doesn't… But he had you… What about the contract?" Then her thoughts started again, her mind racing at top speed. "What does this mean for the military alliance? For the trade routes and oil prices? My country is counting on it. My people. Your people. The wedding *has* to go forward." She said it, and she believed it with a burning conviction even while her emotions, her heart, her very soul, rejoiced at the thought of not having to marry Hassan.

"You will still marry the ruler of Umarah. But Hassan has decided to step down. He is in love with his mistress and she is carrying his child. Under those circumstances, he has decided he must do what is best for his growing family."

Heat prickled her arms, the back of her neck. "Who is the new ruler of Umarah? Who am I meant to marry now?"

"You will marry me, *amira*. I am the new High Sheikh of Umarah."

CHAPTER NINE

THERE was no triumph in his voice. No warmth. Nothing to signal that the news he was delivering was positive or negative in any way. It simply was. But that was Adham's way. If something needed to be done, he did it. He picked up the slack when others failed. He came through when others fell short. It was who he was.

"So now might be a good time to explain your relationship to Hassan, then," she said, her throat tight and dry like sandpaper.

"He is my brother. Older by two years."

"I thought your family had been killed."

"All but Hassan and myself. He is the only family I have left."

The knife of guilt that had been sticking sharply into her ribs twisted again. He was not simply Adham's friend, he was his brother. That made those stolen moments at the oasis seem even worse.

"Why didn't you just tell me?" There were a lot of other questions she needed to ask, a lot of other bases to cover, but she had to know that first.

"That I was Hassan's brother? Because I wanted to gain your trust, and I knew that would not happen if you knew of my relationship to him."

"So you lied to me?"

"And we both cheated."

She knew instinctively that it didn't matter if she was no longer marrying Hassan. What had happened between them was still an aberration in Adham's eyes. The sin had been committed, and it was not forgiven. And she knew that he would never forget her part in it, or his.

"Yes. We can't take it back, though."

"No. But we will move forward."

"And you're intent on marrying me in order to honor the contract?"

"I said that I would."

She remembered the conversation they'd had on the street in Paris—a conversation that seemed as though it had taken place in another lifetime. He'd said he didn't want to marry, but that if he had to, if others were dependent on him doing so, he would. She had become to him what Hassan had been to her. It made her feel sick.

"Yes. You did."

"The country is going to be shaken by this. Hassan is a beloved leader, and though I have served Umarah all my life the people don't know me well. That is by design. It is easiest for me to conduct my duty if I'm not high-profile. But that will make this transition difficult."

Isabella took a breath. "I'll do what I can to help it go smoothly."

"Our marriage will help. The Umarahn people were expecting you as their Sheikha."

"There isn't a better man to rule than you, Adham. I'm certain of that. You have given everything for your country, for your people…"

"I think I have proven that I am as capable of weakness as anyone else."

She could tell it physically hurt him to say it—that the words scraped raw as they left his throat.

"You're not weak, Adham," she whispered.

"I never will be again."

There was finality in his tone—a coldness that chilled her straight to the bone.

"Hassan and Jamilah are leaving tomorrow. We will stay here while we prepare a formal announcement of the passing on of leadership and our wedding," he said.

"We won't go back to the city?"

"Not yet. We will marry in the city, but until then we will stay here. We will be closer to some of the Bedouin encampments, and it would be best if we were to go and visit them. Too often they feel as though they are on the fringe, and yet they're very much a part of our country. I would have them feel as important as they are."

Isabella's heart swelled. Pride, she realized. Because, whether or not this was what Adham had envisioned for himself, he was born to lead. And she would have to find her place. Figure out where she fit, what she could do to help him.

Although she had a feeling he would rather her place were far away from him. The gulf between them had only widened since they'd made love. That moment of closeness—that brief, burning instant that she'd spent in the center of the sun—had been an illusion. And she was paying the price for it. She had lost any real link she'd had with Adham.

He turned to go, and without thinking she put her hand on him, desperate to find some sort of connection with him. "You aren't staying?"

He turned, his eyebrows locked together, his jaw tense, the muscle of his forearm beneath her hand tight. "I have my own quarters. You will stay in yours."

His words—harsh, final—were like a physical slap.

"And after the wedding?" she asked, despising herself for the hopeful note in her voice.

"That will depend on whether or not you are pregnant. We didn't take any precautions."

She nodded, feeling sick to her core. Now that she had given herself to him he didn't want her at all. Now that she would be forced to marry him, live with him for the rest of her life, he despised her. Living with Hassan while loving Adham would have been less torturous than having Adham while his heart was locked tightly away from her—being his wife while he didn't desire her at all.

When he left, closing the door behind him, she sat on the bed, her eyes dry and stinging, her pain too acute for tears. She felt brittle, as though the life was being drained from her.

It was one thing to be denied a life with Adham. But to be given a life with him and have him withhold himself from her...she did not know how she could live with that.

Adham swept a shaking hand over his forehead, disgusted with himself for how hard it was to deny Isabella. Even now he wanted her, after having possessed her only a few short hours ago.

Everything in his life had suddenly changed. All the things he had never desired—a wife, family, becoming High Sheikh—were thrust upon him, and still his most pressing need seemed to be for Isabella's ripe body.

He despised the weakness in himself. Despised that she had such control over him—a control he could not seem to regain.

Until he could, he would not allow himself to touch her. He had a country to think of. His duty extended beyond simply protecting borders and rooting out threats. He was now responsible for everything. And he would do it—would do the best thing possible for his people, as he had done during his years of military service.

He would marry Isabella. But he would not allow her to lead him around by vulnerable body parts. He had never given a woman such power over him. Women were women—easy to find and interchangeable. Sex, no matter how much he enjoyed it, was only sex. It was an easy thing for a man of wealth and power to get, should he want it.

Though he knew he would not find another woman. Not now that he was going to marry Isabella. He would be faithful to her, as he would demand faithfulness of her.

But first he had to gain control of the wild heat that seemed to overcome him when he was in her presence.

The next morning Adham sat at the head of the breakfast table, preparing a formal announcement, while Hassan and his mistress sat in the middle, the woman's eyes downcast, Hassan avoiding Isabella's gaze. Isabella was seated at the end, with aides and servants buzzing around her, the conversation in rapid Arabic moving too quickly for her to follow.

She put her head down and concentrated on eating her hot cereal. She couldn't imagine a more awkward moment. And she'd never felt more like a commodity than she did right then, with Hassan sitting next to the woman of his choice, caressing her tenderly, making sure she was well. And there *she* was, sitting leagues away from her new fiancé—the fiancé who didn't want her, who wouldn't even look at her. Who had inherited her as part of a package deal with his new kingdom.

Her ears perked up, picking up the word *wedding* when spoken by Adham's deep voice. "I see no reason it should not take place as planned."

Hassan nodded. "It will give the people a sense of security."

Oh, good. She was a security blanket for the people.

She sighed. It seemed ridiculous that she had been prepared for this with Hassan, but that now it was Adham it seemed…worse. Worse because she actually wanted Adham, because she loved him, and because she knew he was now stuck in a life, a position, he had not wanted. And she was a part of that.

She loved the man, and seeing him now, seated at the head of the table, going through massive stacks of paperwork, was like watching a tiger that had been caged. Adham would be a wonderful king. The best. And yet it was not what he had wanted for himself. And hadn't he given enough?

She was just another sacrifice he was being forced to make.

"Isabella, where is your ring?" Adham spoke directly to her for the first time since she'd sat down at the table.

She flexed her fingers. "Oh… I thought that…" She looked at Hassan, then back to Adham. "It seemed inappropriate."

"The ring was designed specifically for you by the palace jeweler."

Designed for her? By whose standards? Her mother's? Her father's? The ring was a brilliant solitaire, beautiful in its perfection, but it had nothing whatsoever to do with her as a person. And it had been Hassan's ring. She wanted Adham's. More than that she wanted his heart. He didn't seem prepared to give her either, or even understand why it might be important.

For the first time Jamilah spoke. "You can't expect Isabella to wear a ring that was given to her by another man."

"Actually," Isabella said crisply, "it was delivered to me by courier. So I suppose it's impersonal enough that it should not matter."

"But it does," Jamilah insisted. "Men are foolish when it comes to such matters."

On that she could wholeheartedly agree with her. And, since Jamilah was to be her sister-in-law, she was glad that she and the other woman had something other than a fiancé in common.

Hassan cleared his throat. "Yes, men are foolish. It takes us extra time to see what we truly need sometimes."

Isabella felt her heart squeeze tight, seeing the love that passed between Hassan and Jamilah. Isabella blinked back hot tears and cleared her throat. Seeing Hassan in love, seeing the way he looked at Jamilah…it brought to light just how far she was from that place with Adham.

She stood, pushing her bowl back, tired of the pretense of enjoying breakfast while life swirled around her, out of her control. "I'm finished. Nice to meet you, Jamilah."

She turned and walked from the room, unable to say anything to Adham for fear she might break down entirely. Everything should feel perfect now. She was marrying the man she loved. But it wasn't perfect. It was a mockery of her feelings. The man she loved was being forced into a union with her, and being a part of his unhappiness was worse than not having him at all.

A gentle touch on her shoulder stopped her. "Isabella." It was Jamilah, her liquid dark eyes full of concern. "I hope that you are all right, Isabella. I know what it's like to lose the man you love…or to think you will. I would hate it if you were heartbroken over this."

She let out a watery laugh. "I'm not. I'm very happy for both of you," she said, choked. "I would have hated to be the cause of your separation."

Jamilah looked down. "I resented you, Isabella. How could I not? You were going to marry the man I loved, the father of my child, and I had no argument against it. I still don't. Now Adham has had to give up his life too, and you have been shuffled around like a commodity…"

"Don't feel guilty. Adham and I… I would rather be with Adham."

A smile lit Jamilah's beautiful face. "Then this is a *good* thing for you! For both of you."

Isabella laughed, the sound hollow and brittle in the empty corridor. "I don't know if it's good for both of us but…I care for him."

"It's a good start," the other woman offered.

"I suppose." She left out the fact that Adham resented her, that he felt she was responsible for revealing some sort of weakness in him. She didn't need a big loud confrontation with him to know that.

With Adham, the silences were the worst. That icy, indifferent expression that he was so good at projecting was more cutting than angry words could ever be. It was in the small things, like the ring, that he showed just how little she mattered.

"Hassan and I are leaving the country for a while. Until everything dies down. He's concerned for my health…the health of the baby."

What must it be like to have a man care like that? Adham had always protected her, but he had protected her because it was the right thing to do. In that sense duty was entirely inadequate. Just as it was a wholly awful reason for the man you loved to marry you.

The door to the dining room swung open and Adham and Hassan came into the corridor. Adham's eyes locked with hers, the dark fire there igniting a heat that burned slowly in her. Desire, need, and a longing so intense it made her want to weep with it. It wasn't just a physical need, a physical desire. She wanted his love. She wanted it so badly that it hurt.

But the man standing in front of her, the man with scars that ran deep, with roots buried in his heart, would never love her.

He did come to her side and take her arm, the gesture traditional, proprietary and devoid of anything personal. It hurt worse than the distance.

"We will see you when you return for the wedding," Adham said, gripping his brother's hand.

"Thank you for this, Adham. And you, Isabella."

She didn't know what to say to that. So she only nodded, pressure building in her chest until she was certain the dam would burst and her tears would flood the massive palace.

Hassan put his arm around Jamilah's waist and led her down the corridor, away from Adham and herself.

"I am happy for them," she said quietly as they moved out of sight.

"It is the right thing for Hassan to do. When a child is involved... Consideration has to be given to that."

"What about to him and Jamilah? To the fact that they love each other?"

"What does love matter, Isabella? The kind of love between men and women, lust, that fades with time? It is easily broken, abandoned for a thousand insignificant reasons every day. But a marriage that serves a purpose, that is bigger than the two people involved, *that* marriage has a chance."

"So you don't believe that Hassan and Jamilah will stay together?"

"They have their child. I believe that will bond them."

"But not their feelings for each other?"

"It doesn't matter."

"It does matter. Are you saying you don't believe in love?"

His expression calmed, his eyes suddenly looking beyond her. "You remember, Isabella, we talked about life experience. I have had my share. I have seen much of people—of what the human heart is capable of. Immense greed, unimaginable cruelty. Those things choke love out, kill it where it grows. I have not seen that elusive emotion conquer anything, but I have seen it used against people. I believe love has the power to weaken."

"That's terribly sad, Adham."

"You're young, Bella. You see life as full of wonderful possibilities because you have been given protection by your family—protection from the ugliness in life. But love did not save my parents, Isabella. Do you know, the men that killed my parents…they did not see my mother hiding in the garden, not at first. They used my father to draw her out. Used her love for him, exploited it."

"Adham…" Her voice cracked.

"She could have survived if she had used her mind instead of her heart. No matter what, they were not going to free my father. There was nothing she could have done, and in the end they were both killed."

She saw now where Adham's rigid control, his seeming absence of emotion, came from. He felt it necessary for survival—for the survival of others. And he had honed those defenses, made them so solid, so impenetrable, that she had no hope of breaching them.

"What if it were Hassan? Wouldn't you try to save him?"

"It is different. It is my duty to protect Hassan. I am trained to do so."

She wanted so badly to go to him, to wrap her arms around him and offer him the comfort of her body, offer him whatever he needed. But she stayed still, rooted to the spot, unable to face the rejection that would come if she made a move toward him.

"There is an event this evening," he said, changing the subject suddenly. "Other sheikhs, leaders of some of the larger tribal groups, are coming to the palace. I am to hear their concerns for their communities, listen to their needs, You will attend, of course."

"Of course," she said dryly.

"You will find suitable clothing laid out for you on your bed." He did not look at her when he said that.

Anger flashed through her. "So you're going to choose my clothing now?"

"Clothing that fits the event, your position, the customs of your new country. You may wear what you like in other circumstances."

It was a small concession, but one that meant something to her.

"Thank you."

"I'm not a tyrant, Isabella."

"I know that."

"Then don't look at me as though you expect me to be."

"Do you want honesty, Adham? I don't know what to think. I don't know where we stand, or how you will want your wife to behave. I don't know what you want from me."

He looked at her, his gaze assessing. "I'll give you honesty, since you gave it to me. I don't want a wife. But I do want to do what is best for my people, for your people. That is as far as my expectations of you will go. Otherwise you're free to do as you like."

She had a feeling he looked on that as a gift of some kind, as though he had handed her freedom. But it was impossible. Hearing that he didn't want her hurt worse than she had imagined it would. She hadn't thought that the verbal confirmation would be more difficult to handle than the physical signs, but it was. Much worse.

"I know you'll do what's best for everyone, Adham," she said tightly. "You always do."

"Not always."

"Well, that's done now. We can't go back. And there's no point in dwelling on it now."

"I don't intend to repeat my mistakes."

He strode away, and she stood, rooted to the spot. She was a mistake? Even now that they were going to be married she was nothing more than a mistake?

He had said they would see if she was pregnant or not. Did that mean he only intended to sleep with her to ensure that she produced an heir? When she'd faced marriage to Hassan she would have welcomed that, but with Adham…the thought of him coming to her bed out of duty…

She dashed away the tears that were falling down her cheeks and went to her room. She had to pick one of her pre-selected outfits so that she would be ready to present herself as a proper sheikha. Present herself as a woman her fiancé might be proud to have on his arm.

* * *

Adham disliked state functions. Diplomacy was not his strong point, as he had been told more than once since childhood. He shifted, trying to ignore the discomfort he always experienced when wearing the traditional Umarahn robes. He preferred Western-style clothing to the billowing garb of his ancestors, but meeting with tribal leaders required him to observe tradition in a way he was not accustomed to.

One thing he did discover was that he enjoyed talking to the people. Enjoyed finding out what their needs were, and knowing that he could help them with those needs in an immediate fashion. Being the High Sheikh would have many rewards, but the sacrifices were great. Already he chafed for the freedom of the desert. But that way of living was past.

His future bride was late—a fact he was grateful for. He had not found any more control over his libido since leaving her earlier that day. He still ached for her.

He turned his attention to the Sheikh of one of the larger nomadic groups, who was talking about a need for traveling schools, finding better ways to transport water. That was when he spotted a flash of red out of the corner of his eye and looked up.

Isabella was standing in the doorway of the throne room, her exquisite body draped in rich silk, her dark hair left loose, strands of silver chain woven through it, adding an ethereal shimmer to her glossy black locks. Her eyes were darkened with black kohl, her lips red to match her gown. The style was traditional and modest, yet on her... She looked like the essence of temptation, a call to sin that any man would be hard pressed to resist.

As she moved across the room the heads of every tribal leader turned sharply, their eyes fixed on her womanly form as she walked toward him. Her hips swayed, an enticing rhythm, and her eyes were full of sensual promise.

And she was his.

Mine.

She didn't offer him a smile as she came to join him. Her expression was neutral, much more guarded than he was used to seeing. He had hurt her earlier, with his admission that he did not want a wife. But she had to understand that he would not be the sort of husband to her that Hassan would have been.

He would be faithful, and he would give her children. But he did not know how to give the love of a husband. The love of a father. She and her children deserved both, and it galled him to know that he could not give it. Had it been up to him he would have spared her, but the need for their marriage remained. Which meant that she had to sacrifice more than she might have.

But hurting her in that way…it had made him ache to see her eyes so full of pain.

He put his hand on her lower back and felt her stiffen beneath his touch. She had not done that in a long while. She had grown to enjoy his touch, and now she recoiled from it. His body took it as a challenge when it should be pleased. He needed distance, needed time for whatever enchantment she had woven around him to wear off before he went to her bed again.

He raised his hand and the room fell silent, awaiting his word. "This is my future bride—your future Sheikha. Principessa Isabella Rossi. The union between she and I will bring about an alliance with Turan that will benefit both countries." He continued, outlining all that each nation stood to gain from the marriage, while the sheikhs looked on, nodding their heads in approval.

Isabella offered the onlookers a wide smile—one he

suddenly wished were directed at him. Then she did something no other sheikha would have done. "I am honored to be in your service," she said. "Umarah is a wonderful country, and I look forward to learning all that I can about my new home. Thank you for welcoming me."

He did not know what the response would be to a woman speaking, but the men only nodded, clapping and laughing at the end of her speech.

Afterward, they spoke to Isabella as well as to him, telling her specifically about the needs of the women and children in their groups.

When they sat down to dinner Isabella took her place at his side. "You should smile more," she whispered—the first words she'd spoken to him all evening.

"I should?"

"I've told you that before." Conversation and music swirled, loud and boisterous around them, as food was placed on the table.

"I don't know that the people expect their High Sheikh to smile."

"It's always better to talk to someone who smiles than someone who simply glares at you."

"I don't glare."

"Yes, Adham, you do."

"Do I glare at you?"

"All the time." A smile tugged the corner of her gorgeous red mouth. He was glad to see it—glad to see her smile again instead of that blank, serious expression. Perhaps that was what she felt when he smiled. A sense of pride, as though she had accomplished something.

"I will try not to."

She reached her hand up and touched his forehead,

as though she were smoothing out the lines. "I think it's permanent."

He gripped her hand, moved it to his cheek, held it there. The look in her eyes changed, her pupils expanding, the pulse in her wrist fluttering fast beneath his fingers. An answering pulse pounded in his groin, his body hardening for her.

He dropped her hand, disgusted with himself. That he could get an erection in a room full of people, at an important political event, only told him just how badly he was failing at regaining his control. Never before had a woman distracted him from the task at hand. But Isabella near…her skin so soft, her scent tantalizingly sweet, that lush body that he knew was so tight, that fit him so perfectly, close enough for him to touch, to taste…was a temptation he was not able to combat.

He turned his attention to the man next to him and began discussing mundane tax laws—anything to tone down his body's reaction to his future Sheikha.

Isabella had every man in the room eating out of the palm of her hand by the end of the evening, and as the men filed out they all bowed—a show of reverence and submission rarely given to women—offering her hospitality should she ever be traveling near their encampments.

She was a valuable political asset—something he had not fully appreciated about her when he had first met her. He had assumed she was immature, had thought her youthful enthusiasm would be a drawback, and yet he saw now that that wasn't the case. She was naive, yes, but that only added to her charm, made her seem disarming and sweet, and her enthusiasm, her ready smile, made people want to be with her, talk to her.

No matter who she was conversing with she gave them

all of her focus, all of her attention, and she did it with such an air of interest that whoever she was speaking to felt at the center of her universe. She was an asset that most politicians would dream of.

She leaned against the doorframe, exhaustion evident on her face. She looked so beautiful there, the light from the palace making a halo around her dark hair from behind, the moon casting a silver glow on her golden skin. There was still a lingering warmth in the night air, the scent of sun on sand not yet faded.

"Where did you learn to work a room like that?" he asked.

She shrugged, not looking at him, keeping her eyes fixed on a distant point out in the desert; that unusual reserve that she seemed to be showing only to him was back. "We held many diplomatic events in Turan, and traveled to several outside of the country. I told you, I speak many languages and I often conversed with dignitaries in attendance. I was trained to be a royal wife."

"And you were trained well."

"Yes. I was. I enjoy that part of it, really. I like people. I like hearing about their lives, their dreams and struggles. One thing I've found is that people usually want the same things, no matter how different they are."

"I have never spent a lot of time getting to know people," he said, realizing how true it was.

Other than Hassan, he didn't count anyone as his friend. He'd had affairs with women over the years—nothing permanent, nothing serious. And he hadn't wanted those connections. Hadn't wanted to be close to anyone. Yet Isabella seemed to want to know anyone and everyone. She was so open, so exposed to anyone who might try and hurt her.

"I don't know that I've really gotten to know very

many people. Being royalty, it seems like you're always…
separate. But I've gotten to be a small part of a lot of
people's lives. I like that."

"I thought you were very selfish when we first met,"
he said, remembering how he had assumed she was a
spoiled little rich girl, whining about moving from one
palace to the next. "But that was the only moment in your
life you've ever spared for yourself, wasn't it?"

She laughed softly, a small amount of warmth returning to her face. "I did sneak out shopping with my sister-
in-law once. She didn't know we were sneaking, poor
thing. That turned out to be a bad idea too."

"You think now that your time in Paris was a bad
idea?"

"I don't know, Adham. I learned to want a lot more
than I did before I left. Different things than I thought I
wanted."

"Freedom from the an arranged marriage?"

She pushed away from the doorframe, her eyes, which
had been avoiding him, locked onto him now. "No. I
learned to want things I had ignored—things I had never
thought I would truly desire. How could I when my husband had been chosen for me? There was never a reason
to look at another man, never a reason to want to know
about…sex."

She touched his arm, the brush of her skin sending
a shock of kinetic energy through him, straight to his
groin, making him totally hard in an instant.

"Being with you…that was when I learned what it
was to want." She licked her lips and lust kicked him.
Hard. "That was the other moment in my life when I was
selfish," she finished on a whisper.

He gripped her wrist, backed her against the door, his
mouth finding the sensitive curve of her neck, pressing

a kiss to her flesh, damp from the heat, tasting the salt of her skin, the essence of Isabella. His Bella. *His*.

A small moan escaped her lips and he caught it with his mouth, kissing her hard, devouring her. And she met him, her tongue thrusting into his mouth, her body moving against him, the restrictive fit of her red gown keeping her movements slight.

She tried to spread her legs wider, tried to move that sensitive part of her body against his hardened erection, to give them both the release they so desperately craved. Desire burned in him, wild, uncontrolled.

He gripped her hip, running his hand around to the curve of her bottom and down to her thigh, taking hold of the intricate beaded design on the gossamer fabric and tugging hard, tearing the material so that she was able to move with more freedom. She bent her knee and he lifted her leg, wrapping it around his calf as she leaned back against the doorframe, moving her body sensually against him.

He was ready to come then and there—from her delighted moans of pleasure, from the slick of her tongue against his, from the heat that radiated at the apex of her thighs, a heat that he knew signaled her readiness for him. One more decisive tear of that demure dress and he could sweep it aside and thrust into her...

"Apologies..." A nervous voice brought him out of his sensual haze and he moved away from Isabella, turning to see a young man standing in the corridor, his eyes downcast. "Sheikh Hassan is on the phone and wishes to speak to you."

He looked at Isabella, who had pressed herself tightly to the doorframe, her eyes squeezed shut, her cheeks flushed pink, her breasts rising and falling with each heavy breath she took. Her dress was torn from her thigh down past her knee, revealing smooth golden skin—skin he'd had his hands on only moments ago, that he wanted to have his hands on again. Even now, with a servant standing there looking on, he wanted to finish what they had started. What they had started in a public place in the palace while they were still unmarried.

The Umarahn people would expect a certain code of conduct from their High Sheikh and his Sheikha, and while most of the modern people would assume they were not abstaining, they would still find it distasteful to know that he had nearly taken Isabella against the palace wall, with doors opened to the desert.

No more distasteful than they would find it that he had taken her virginity on the floor of a tent in the middle of the desert while she'd been engaged to their beloved Hassan.

"Goodnight, Isabella," he said, turning away from her.

He heard a sharp catch in her breathing, knew she was holding back a sob, but he kept walking. He could not afford to let her control him—could not afford to let his need for her get so out of hand that he forgot everything for the pursuit of the pleasure he could find in her body. He could not afford to lose focus even for a moment.

He had seen the damage it could cause. And he wanted no part of something that could be that destructive.

CHAPTER TEN

"Again you do not have your ring on." Adham's deep voice was full of censure.

Isabella looked away from the scenery, flying by in a red blur out the window of the Hummer, and down at her bare hand. "What does it matter?"

"It matters a great deal. You are my fiancée. It is expected for you to wear my ring."

She took a deep breath, pain lancing her. "But it isn't your ring. It's Hassan's. And it isn't *my* ring. There's nothing about it that has any personal meaning or value to me."

"You're being petulant."

"Maybe." She wasn't, though. He was just being too obtuse to see it. Because the engagement meant nothing to him. It meant nothing to him that her ring had been a part of an entirely different engagement, that it had been given to her by a delivery man.

It mattered to her, though. It would matter to any woman. It wasn't as though Adham hadn't had relationships before. He should know enough about women to figure that out. Or maybe his affairs had been so detached that he really didn't have a clue what something like a ring could really mean to a woman.

That thought made her feel both relief and heartrending sadness. Relief because she didn't like the idea of Adham's heart having belonged to any other woman, but sadness because the thought of him involving himself in such a soulless, purely physical affair made her almost sick. He was worth so much more than that.

He took one hand off the steering wheel and gripped her wrist, holding her arm up as if he was examining it. "You aren't putting it on."

"I left it back at the palace. I took it off when things were ended with Hassan."

"The engagement, the original arrangement, is still in place."

"Only the fiancé has changed. An incidental, I guess?"

He didn't respond to that. He set her hand gently in her lap, the touch sending a shockwave through her as it always did, and turned his focus back to the road.

"The people at the Bedouin encampment might wonder," he said tightly.

"Then they can wonder. I think it's safe to say that everyone in Umarah knows we have an unusual situation. They know I was promised to Hassan, and they know he's now chosen someone else and that I am marrying his brother. I highly doubt anyone expects our relationship to appear conventional."

"The faster we can erase the scandal from the minds of the people, the better. I see no point in drawing it out. It will all be forgotten eventually. The more we are seen together, the more natural all of this will seem. Then there will be the wedding, and children. None of this will matter."

"So we're putting on a show for the nation? Hoping they'll forget the truth?"

"What does it benefit our people to see tension between

us? We're building an alliance between nations through our marriage. Our union must appear strong, so that they will believe the alliance is strong."

"Much easier that it appear strong than actually have it *be* strong," she muttered, turning her focus back to the arid desert.

"The situation is what it is, Bella. It is not ideal, but we must make the best of it."

Pain shot through her. Not ideal. Well, maybe that was true for him. She *knew* it was true for him. But what did he think it was like for her? Did he really think she would rather be with Hassan? Did he believe that she had given herself to him that night in the desert out of rebellion? How could he be dense enough to miss how much she felt for him?

It came back to the way he saw relationships. The way he saw sex. Sex was recreation for him, affairs a simple diversion in between assignments or work in the oil fields. While for her...it had been life-altering. Being with him like that. Even now it sent a thrill through her body and caused tears to form in her eyes.

Shimmering waves of heat parted in the distance, and Isabella could see oil rigs against the backdrop of the faded blue sky.

Adham gestured to the right, to a mountainous stretch beyond the flat portion where the rigs were stationed. "The encampment is back there. Many of the men work on the fields, adding new joints, checking core samples, measuring depth."

"And the drilling projects were your doing?"

"We were already drilling, but I made the move to invest more in the operation. It's provided good jobs for our people, and a very valuable export. The benefits for the economy have been exponential."

"Really, Adham, is there anything you can't do?"

She turned to look at him, saw his jaw clench, his shoulders roll forward slightly as he tightened his grip on the steering wheel. "I don't know that I have you figured out."

It was such an honest, frustrated admission, one that shocked her. "I can't wear Hassan's ring," she blurted.

"You don't like it?"

"It's a beautiful ring. It's not my style, but it *is* beautiful. I can't wear it because I'm not marrying Hassan. It's linked to him, not to you, and as long as I wear it I feel...I feel like I'm still engaged to him."

"Why couldn't you just say that?" He sounded even more exasperated now.

"Because if I say it, it doesn't mean as much as if you just...figure it out."

"That's ridiculous."

"It isn't," she insisted. "It's like having to ask for flowers."

"Which isn't good either?"

"No. You want the other person to think of it, otherwise it has no meaning."

They were getting close to the rigs now. The sound of drilling filled the air, overpowering the sound of the car's motor, the scent of the crude oil coming through the air vents. The road they were on wound around the rigs, taking them behind the mountains, which did a good job of absorbing the bulk of the noise.

"Life would be simpler if you would just ask for things," he muttered.

"That's very male of you," she said stiffly. The pragmatic side of him reminded her of her brother, and her brother's pragmatic side irritated her.

"Well, *amira*, I am very male." That last comment hung between them as silence filled up the car.

She swallowed, her throat dry. "Yes." She knew that. She knew that so very well.

That one time together, though…had it only been two days ago?…hadn't been enough. She hadn't gotten to see enough of his body, hadn't had enough opportunity to simply admire his physique, to enjoy the feel of his hot skin against hers.

Her face flamed.

It was strange to think she'd actually slept with him. She'd imagined, when she'd even let herself think about it, that sex would bring people closer together, not make everything so…complicated.

Maybe it wasn't really complicated. She knew how she felt about him, and he'd made it clear how he felt about her. So it was just sad, then.

A row of low, dark tents came into view, and Isabella could see smoke rising from campfires, children running around with their mothers close behind them. Out here in the middle of the desert, with all of the sand so still, there was life.

"I can't believe they live out here. There's nothing for so many miles."

"It's their way of life. They've lived this way for centuries. We do the best we can to provide mobile medical service."

"What about emergencies?" she asked, looking at the children.

"We do the best we can. Many of the Bedouin encampments have satellite phones and generators now that enable them to call, and we can have helicopters sent if necessary."

"And schools?"

"Something that hasn't been handled to my satisfaction yet," he said, bringing the car to a halt on the outskirts of the camp.

She unbuckled quickly and let herself out of the vehicle, meeting him halfway around the other side. "Do you have any ideas?"

"Not any that are feasible at the moment, but it's something that Hassan was working on, and I'm happy to continue that work and see it through."

"Definitely. Education is so important."

"I didn't know you were so passionate about it."

"I am. Without the schooling I had…" She tried to think of a way to explain it. "It was my escape. I learned about what I couldn't do, places I couldn't go. It added so much to my life. Every child…every person…should have that."

Adham looked at Isabella, at the passion in her blue eyes as she spoke, and his respect for her grew. She was much more complex than he'd given her credit for when he'd first met her. He'd thought she was simply spoiled and immature, but that wasn't it. She was naive, but she was smart. Innocent in the ways of the world, but savvy in social situations.

And having *his* ring meant something to her. That was an intriguing thing. He hadn't imagined it would matter to her. It was still an arranged marriage—a marriage she didn't want but was willing to go through with for the sake of her country, just as he was.

Now that he knew, he wanted to ensure she had a ring she would love. A ring that fit her. He had no idea why it suddenly mattered, except that it mattered to *her*. Isabella should have some happiness, should have something she wanted.

The wind blowing through the camp was hot, and they

got a blast of it when they moved away from the car and began walking toward the camp. Isabella licked her lips, and he felt the impact of it hard in his gut. He wanted her—wanted her with a ferocity that nearly drove him to grab her and haul her back to the Hummer, so he could take her in the back seat, feel the tight, wet heat of her body around him again.

His hands shook with his need. This...this desire that was so all-consuming it was like a weed. It had taken root, and now it had gone so deep he couldn't extract it.

No. He would. She was to be his wife, and wanting her was expected—welcome. But he could not allow it to control him.

The leader of the Bedouin tribe walked out to greet them, children clustering around him, their eyes round with awe over meeting such a powerful man. Isabella imagined they had no real idea that Adham was the king, but they didn't really need to. Adham projected power effortlessly. In a group, he would be the one others would turn to for guidance automatically, even without a title connected to him.

A rush of pride filled her as she watched him—the man she loved, the man she was going to marry—walk with the other man over to the fire and sit with all the men, talking with them, treating them like equals, listening to their concerns. She knew Adham hadn't been comfortable at the big, formal event that had been held at the palace, but here he was in his element. Connected to his people.

One of the women ushered her into the tent where they were sitting, talking and laughing, sewing in the lantern light. She loved talking to them, finding out about their customs, hearing stories about their children.

They had so little, and yet they had so much love. It was how Isabella wanted to treat her children—the children she would have with Adham. She wanted them to have more than nannies and tutors. She wanted them to have this. Love. Acceptance. For them to know she was proud of them. She wanted them to have everything her parents had denied her.

When Adham came into the tent a couple of hours later Isabella's heart leapt into her throat at the sight of him. He made sure he greeted all the women, even taking time to ask for each of their names.

Then he turned to her. "It is time for us to go, Isabella."

She nodded and stood, and he placed his hand on the small of her back. The gesture was intended as a casual maneuver, and she knew that, but it still sent reckless heat blazing through her, made her feel as though she was on fire with her desire for him. Even in front of people it was like that. And he, as always, was a statue, never betraying a moment's discomfort, not affected in the least.

When they were back in the car, Isabella leaned toward the passenger door, trying to put some distance between the two of them.

"Did you enjoy making conversation with the women?" he asked.

She nodded. "Yes. We had some time to discuss the difficulties with schooling out here..." She hesitated. "I think...I think I have an idea."

"Do you?" He didn't sound condescending, as her father would have, he actually sounded interested. That bolstered her confidence.

"Yes. I was thinking that we could do a simple 'six weeks on, six weeks off' schedule and bring teachers in on rotation. That way the children would get the education they need, but a teacher who isn't accustomed to living out here won't burn out from living in the desert for so long at a time."

"That's a good idea."

"You think so?"

"Yes. We had thought of boarding schools, but the more traditional people want their children home, so that they can also educate them according to their customs. But having the teachers here, on a schedule that would allow them breaks, would probably be the best solution. I'll talk to the teachers we have out in the field and work at tailoring a schedule with them."

Isabella couldn't hold back her smile. She liked that she had been able to at least offer one solution to Adham. Especially since she was the cause of so many of his problems.

That thought made her smile fade again.

"We have more tribal leaders coming to the palace tomorrow. They are less…modern than some of the men we've met so far. They will not wish you to be present when we meet."

"Oh." She didn't know what else to say to that.

"I have always been proud of my father's legacy, of Hassan's, of what they have done to champion women's rights in our country, but these people…they live in the heart of the desert, untouched by technology or many other things from the modern world."

"I see." It hurt her feelings to be told she wasn't wanted. Of course it did. Even if it was silly. It wasn't as though Adham had said *he* didn't want her around.

But he didn't. That was why it bothered her. Because she felt as if he was using the wishes of the tribal leaders to get rid of her.

It would help if she could tell what he was thinking. But she couldn't. She never could.

"I wish I could read your mind," she said, not really intending to say it out loud, but not sorry she had.

"No," he said, his voice rough suddenly. "You don't wish that."

"Yes. I do. You said to ask for what I wanted. I wish I could understand you. We're going to get married. I think it would be helpful if we at least reached some sort of understanding."

He applied the brakes, stopping the car in the middle of the desert road and turning to her, his eyes glittering in the dim light. "If you could read my thoughts you would be scandalized."

"Maybe I'd like to be scandalized."

"I think you and I have caused enough scandal."

"We can't dwell on that forever. What happened that night happened. There's nothing that can be done about it now."

He extended his hand, cupped her cheek, and she realized that he was shaking. His eyes were intense on hers, his mouth set into a hard line, his jaw locked tight. He stroked the line of her jaw with his thumb.

When he kissed her, it was hot and hard, fierce but short, his lips burning her, searing her soul.

Adham reveled in the touch of her soft lips, enjoyed the velvet feel of the inside of her mouth against his tongue, her taste, her smell, everything uniquely and wholly Isabella. His heart was slamming hard against his chest, all of his blood rushing south of his belt, making him hard, making him ache.

He wanted her—wanted to peel her modest dress off and reveal her breasts to his gaze, to taste those hardened tips, suck them between his lips. He wanted to see all of her, touch all of her, sink into her tight body and lose himself in her, give up the battle he was waging against his own desire.

He wrenched his mouth away from hers, his hands unsteady, his stomach tight, his heart beating in a chest that felt too small to accommodate it.

This was a madness that could not be endured. If he were another man—a man with less responsibility, a man who didn't have two nations of people depending on him—he would take Isabella away and spend however long it took—weeks, months—exorcising her from his system. As it was, he didn't have that time. He was a man who could not afford to have any weakness in him, a man who needed to be strong, who needed to have dominion over his every fleshly need.

And that meant he couldn't afford to give in. Not to any desire that had the power to control him, that had the power to overshadow his good sense. That had the power to make him forget his loyalty to his brother, the only family he had left. Family he had betrayed so easily.

If he could break those bonds of loyalty with his brother, what would prevent him from breaking his vows to Isabella? Breaking the vows of service he'd made to his country?

He had to find his strength again. Find his control.

"This will not happen again until after the wedding," he ground out, satisfied that he had made a decree, that he had set a timeline. One he would follow. One she would follow.

She settled back into her seat, her head tilted back, exposing the smooth line of her elegant throat. Lust gripped him hard, challenged him. He squashed it ruthlessly, shutting off all feeling, all thoughts of anything except for the passing desert.

He was the High Sheikh of Umarah. Ultimate control belonged to him. He would not give in to temptation. She was only a woman—one in a long line of many. He would not allow her to get beneath his defenses again.

CHAPTER ELEVEN

ADHAM was a cold stranger the next morning at breakfast, although the servants and aides were still moving around, talking. It would die down, she supposed. It wasn't so chaotic at the Turani palace, but then, unless it was a formal occasion her father didn't often eat meals with the family. Perhaps if he had there would have been more activity in the dining room.

She wondered if Adham would always take meals in here, with her. With their children. She could be pregnant. It was unlikely, but possible. She wanted Adham's child, but she hoped she hadn't conceived yet. They had way too many issues to work through before adding a child into the mix.

Adham was either hot or cold with her. That was an understatement; he was either blazing or completely frozen. As he was this morning.

When the staff left, only the two of them remained. She hated the awkwardness. At least they'd had some sort of relationship before all of this. It had been tense at times, and they'd often been working toward opposing goals, with the undercurrent of attraction always there, making things difficult, but it hadn't been like this.

He was so closed off, all of his defenses up, his walls

thick around his soul. Keeping her out. Keeping everyone out.

"Do you want children?" she asked, blurting it out before she had a chance to censor herself.

"I need children. An heir."

"But do you *want* them?"

"Do you?"

She thought about it—really thought about it for the first time—about what she would choose if there was no one involved but herself and the man she loved. What it would be like to hold a child in her arms, a baby. The only baby she'd ever held was her niece. She was so perfect, a little mix of Max and Alison. Would their baby be the same? A mix of the two of them? It made her heart tighten, made tears well up in her eyes.

"Yes," she said, knowing it was true. "I had always taken it for granted before that I would but…yes, I do. Even if I weren't in the position I'm in, I would want them."

He didn't respond, he only lowered his eyes to the documents that were in front of him.

"You wouldn't, would you?" she asked, feeling a heavy sickness settle in her stomach.

"I do not want a wife. Why would I want a child?" His voice was hard, cold.

"So if we do have a baby…you won't love him?"

"I will give what I have, Isabella. No child of mine will be neglected."

"Of course," she said slowly, hearing the bitterness creeping into her tone. "You would do your duty. As you always do."

"At least I will do that. Many men do not."

"But is it enough if your relationship with your father is

only there because he feels he has to give it to you?" She knew it wasn't enough from a fiancé, from a husband.

"You're borrowing trouble. There is no child yet."

"But there will be, Adham. We're going to have a family together, and I have a right to know how you see that family in your mind."

He said nothing for a long moment, clenching his fists tightly, like he did when he was grappling with his control. "I wish that I could offer you more."

"You could."

"No, Isabella. I lost that ability long ago. That's what life experience can do to you. It hardens you. You simply haven't been through enough to know that yet."

"You're doing a wonderful job of making sure I reach that point," she said acidly, rising from her chair and exiting the room, her heart pounding in her chest.

She wanted to scream, wanted to run into the solitude of the desert and hurl obscenities at the sky. Why did there have to be such a painful distance between herself and the man she was supposed to marry? The man she loved.

It seemed cruel that in a room full of strangers she could connect, could laugh with them, talk with them, and yet the one man she could not reach was Adham. There was a war raging inside him. She felt it—felt the struggle, the tension in his body whenever they were near each other. She didn't know what he was fighting, and she had even less of an idea of who would win.

But if she could have nothing else she would find a connection with him again. She couldn't stand him being a stranger anymore. She couldn't stand that moment of connection, that moment when he'd been inside her, been one with her, to be nothing more than a distant memory.

She needed more than that. From her marriage. From life. There were choices in her life that had been made for her, things that were out of her control, but she would not let her relationship with her future husband be one of them.

The household was still when Isabella crept from her room that night. The staff had left long ago, the guards that were standing sentry outside silent and out of sight.

She had managed to get directions to Adham's chambers from one of the maids—which had been embarrassing, since the other woman had clearly been shocked that Isabella didn't already know the location of her fiancé's bedroom.

She wrapped her robe more tightly around her body, holding it against her skin like a shield. She was mostly bare beneath it, the only covering under the terrycloth the sheerest bra and panties set she'd bought while she was in Paris.

Pushing the bedroom door open, she walked in and took a deep breath, clenching her hands tight, trying to stop the shaking. The only thing she really feared was his rejection.

"Adham."

That voice—husky and sensual, so sexy—called out to him in his sleep, penetrated his dreams. Adham rolled over and froze. She was there, standing by the door, the pale moonlight bathing her body in a silver glow. Her white robe was bright in the light, and he could see clearly as she unfastened the belt and then shrugged it off her shoulders, letting it fall to the floor, pooling at her feet, leaving herself nearly naked to his gaze.

Even in the dim light he could see the faint shadow

of lacy lingerie, and beneath that the darker shade of her nipples and the curls that covered her feminine mound.

His heart-rate increased. His body was instantly, painfully hard. When she moved forward, those hips swaying, her perfect body moving with such feminine elegance, his whole body burned with a need so acute his teeth ached.

"Bella," he grated.

"Adham," she said again, her voice enough to make his shaft jump. "I need you."

He needed *her*. He had no idea how it had become so. Yes, he needed her in a physical sense, but suddenly it felt like more. It was almost impossible to keep himself in the bed, to keep from getting up and taking her in his arms, holding her to him.

"What happened between us…I know it was wrong. I know why you haven't touched me since. I do understand what a betrayal it was for you. The fault was with me." Her voice sounded thicker now. "But that's behind us now. It has to be. We're getting married. We're the ones who are trying to make a better future for our people. We can't have that night standing between us."

She reached behind her back and her bra straps slid down her shoulders, down her arms, revealing her full breasts. He gripped the sheets, willing himself to stay where he was. He wanted to watch her, wanted to let her lead. A first for him, but he was captivated by her, held captive by his desire for her.

"So, I want us to start again." She gripped the sides of her thong and shimmied out of it, dropping it onto the floor with her bra. And she was naked in front of him, her body, so lush and womanly, the most perfect sight he could imagine.

She put her knee on the bed, then brought her other

leg up so that she was kneeling before him, still out of his reach, but close enough that he could smell her scent. Floral and female, uniquely Isabella.

She gripped the edge of the sheet, pulled it toward her until it slid away from his body, revealing just how much he desired her. Her eyes rounded, her lips parting.

"I didn't get to see you the first time. Not really." She moved forward, her movements more awkward now, but he found that just as sexy.

She wrapped her hand around his erection, a small sound escaping her lips. He couldn't hold back the groan that rumbled in his chest. Her hands were so soft, and she looked so wicked and tempting that he was afraid he might not be able to hold back, that he might end things then and there.

She moved her thumb along his shaft, the motion unpracticed but even more erotic because of it.

"I want…" she began, but her voice deserted her for a moment. "I want to be in control this time."

She leaned forward, flicking her tongue lightly over the head of his penis. He gripped the sheets tighter, the breath hissing through his teeth. He should stop her. He would. *Soon.*

"I've been wanting to do that," she whispered.

Leaning in again, she continued to give him attention with her mouth, her exploration growing bolder as she continued, her noises of pleasure mingling with his.

"Bella," he ground out, feeling the first shiver of orgasm rack his body. "Stop. Now. I can't hold back."

She didn't stop, and he didn't possess enough willpower to make her. He could only wind his fingers through her hair as she continued, taking him deep into her mouth, the moist heat surrounding him, pushing him over into the abyss, waves of pleasure coursing through him, sending molten heat through his veins.

Isabella raised her head, situating herself so that her head rested on his stomach, her glossy black hair spilling over his chest as she moved her hand idly over the ridges of his abdominal muscles, over the hard, smooth flesh, scarred in places, but still so beautiful to her. So alive.

She could feel his heart raging, could tell by the fine sheen of sweat on his body how intensely he had been affected by what had just passed between them. She felt as if she had just won a small victory. For a few moments she had held the control, had made him shake with need, had pushed him over into that place where there was nothing but pleasure, nothing but the moment.

"Come here," he said, his voice husky.

She levered herself up so that her face was even with his, and he cupped her chin, kissed her deeply on the lips before reversing their position so that she was on her back, vulnerable to him now.

His eyes were hot, his pulse beating rapidly at the base of his neck, and she could feel his body hardening again.

Her eyes widened. "You can't be ready again already. I took biology classes, so I do know some things."

He chuckled, a wicked grin spreading across his face. He looked younger, more carefree than she'd ever seen him look, and, even as aroused as she was, she felt tears gather in her eyes.

"Give me a few more minutes," he said, "I'm not quite there yet."

"Then what…? *Oh!*" She let her head fall back onto the pillow as he closed his lips over the tip of her breast, sucking it hard into his mouth.

He pulled away, blowing lightly on her damp skin,

making her nipple harden painfully, before moving down, kissing the rounded curve of her breast, her ribs, her stomach, the tender spot just beneath her belly button.

His teeth grazed her hipbone lightly, the tiny sting of pain mingled with the pleasure roaring through her body was so erotic that she felt the first wave of orgasm begin to rise up, her internal muscles pulsing, ready for his possession.

"Adham," she breathed, reaching for his shoulders, trying to bring him up so that she could kiss him, so that she could have him inside her.

"Not yet, *amira*," he said, parting her legs, pressing a hot kiss to her inner thigh.

She shivered, her body anticipating the touch of his mouth to her most sensitive spot even before he made the move.

When the heat of his tongue did touch her there, sweeping over her clitoris, she arched beneath him, a sharp cry escaping her lips. Was this what he'd felt when she'd done it to him? So helpless and shaky? Desperate for release and feeling as if she was standing on the edge of a cliff?

He pleasured her that way until her entire body was rocking with wave after wave of pleasure, crashing through her, leaving her spent and breathless.

"Was it that good for you?" she asked, her words labored as she tried to catch her breath.

"Better."

"That's impossible."

She was rewarded with another dark chuckle as he moved to take her lips in a searing kiss.

"Now," she pleaded, another climax building inside of her. "Please."

He wrapped his arms around her waist and brought

her down so that she was on top of him, straddling him. He gripped her buttocks with his big hands as he moved her into position, so that his hardness was nudging the entrance of her body.

She sighed as he stretched her, filled her. There was no pain this time, only pleasure so deep, so intense, it seemed impossible for her body to accommodate it.

They moved together, their breathing building in a staccato rhythm, their sighs of ecstasy filling the air, and when they reached the summit this time they went over together.

"I love you." The words fell from her lips with ease, straight from her heart. And even though she hadn't intended to say them she wouldn't call them back. She did love him. With everything she had. He had made her who she was. He had helped her become a woman—not because he'd taken her virginity, but because he had shown her the importance of putting others before herself, the importance of living for more than her own happiness.

He had made her complete. And if he never loved her in return, she would survive. She could never be sorry that she loved him. He was good, strong, the most wonderful man she'd ever known.

Isabella rested her head on his chest, her cheek pressed against the place where his heart was beating, fast and ragged. Her body was satisfied, but her heart wanted to weep with the need to feel as though it had mattered to him, affected him, put a crack in those walls that surrounded him.

She looked at him, at his face, and saw his expression unguarded for the first time. Raw. Confused. And if he had been any other man she might have thought she saw fear there too.

She put her hand on his cheek, moved in to kiss him, but he derailed her, drawing her to him, wrapping her in his embrace and bringing her to rest again on his chest. It was a caring gesture…or at least it appeared to be. But she knew it was his way of regaining control. Of avoiding conversation.

So she let him. And he didn't seem to notice the warm tears that fell from her cheeks onto his bare skin.

His arms were tight around her, but as close as he held her, her breasts crushed to his bare chest, she felt there was a gulf between them. A gulf that was there by his design.

Desperate to find some closeness, a connection, she pressed a kiss to the scar that bisected his pectoral, the light dusting of hair tickling her lips. He stiffened, his muscles locking tight.

"I think it would be best if you went back to your own room, *amira*."

She looked up at him, at his face, closed off and cold. It seemed to come so easily to him. How did he do it? She was rocked to her core, her entire world tilted off of its axis, and he was detached.

Maybe he was right. Maybe he couldn't love. But she had a hard time believing that. He was the best man she had ever known. A man who put others before himself constantly. He had sacrificed his life for his country, continued to do so even now that he was the High Sheikh.

But for all of the goodness in him he was so hard, so damaged, she feared she would never reach his heart. She wanted to. She wanted to tear away those barriers if she had to do it with her bare hands, if she had to dig until her fingers bled. She wanted to reach him. Wanted to find the man beneath all the protective layers.

She wanted to heal him, but he didn't even realize that he was wounded.

"Did I do something wrong?" she asked, sitting up, not bothering to cover her breasts. It was pointless now. She'd already given him so much more than her body that her nudity was the least of her concerns.

"I do not want any of the staff to find you here."

"I don't care."

"Maybe honor and tradition mean nothing to you—"

"That isn't fair, Adham." She climbed out of the bed, unable to be close to him when she felt so angry. "I wasn't alone that night."

"I didn't mention that night."

"But that's what this is about. That's what all of it is about."

"You were the one who said you wanted it put behind us. Yet you bring it up now, when that it suits you to fight."

She wanted to scream in frustration. "Well, maybe I don't know how to handle this. *Any* of this. I'm so…I'm confused. And we just…we just shared that incredible experience and you want me to *leave*!"

His jaw tightened, and there was a dangerous glint in his dark eyes. "Just go, Isabella."

"You can't order me around. I thought you'd learned that by now."

He stood from the bed too, not bothering to cover his body either. His naked physique was enough to make her feel hot, even as angry as she was.

"You are still so young," he said. "You take everything personally, make it about you. I am guarding your reputation. A virgin princess is expected, required by the more traditional citizens of my country, and I will not bring shame to them with ugly rumors of their Sheikha.

Staff are only so loyal when money is offered to give up salacious secrets."

"But we're getting married. It isn't as though—"

"As though we slept together while you were engaged to marry my brother? Do not think we have escaped those sorts of rumors. It is one reason we have stayed here rather than returning to Maljadeed. The press in the city is rabid, and gossip is flying everywhere. Hassan has been open about his desire to marry for love, but our relationship is a source of great interest. I mean to protect your reputation."

"Maybe I don't need you to protect my reputation," she flung out carelessly.

"You feel too much, Bella, with too much passion," he grated.

"And you feel nothing."

He turned away from her, his high cheekbones, the square shape of his jaw highlighted by the moon filtering through the window. "It is better that way."

"I don't think it is."

She swooped down and picked her robe up from the floor, embarrassment hitting as she tugged it on. Somehow dressing in front of him and making the walk of shame out of his bedroom felt much more shameful than disrobing for him had.

But to her it had been an act of love, and to him it had been nothing but satisfying his libido.

It was a strange thing how after sharing that kind of closeness with him she seemed to feel more disconnected in the aftermath.

"That's just more evidence of how naive you are," he said, his voice hard, unyielding.

"I'm not naive, Adham," she said, her voice shaking.

"You've done a very good job of ensuring that I didn't remain that way."

She turned and stalked from the room and Adham watched her go, his heart tight in his chest. She was right. He was ensuring she was no longer naive. He was taking everything that was beautiful in her and destroying it. Poisoning it with the ugliness that tainted his life.

And yet there was no other course of action he could take but to keep her with him. She was to be the Sheikha of Umarah—his wife. She had already proven more effective than him at matters of diplomacy. And it would cost her.

That realization sent a shaft of burning pain through his chest more severe than he could ever remember feeling before. He had been numb there for so long he hadn't imagined himself capable of experiencing that level of feeling. Not anymore.

But Isabella…she made him feel.

I love you.

It was easy to dismiss her declaration. She was young. He was her first lover. And yet, as easy as it would be to use those things to discredit her, the passion, the conviction in her voice, had hit him square in the chest.

He had been shot. Multiple times. Her words had held no less impact than a bullet. They even burned the same.

He didn't want it to burn. He didn't want to feel anything.

Emotions couldn't be trusted. His people needed a leader—someone who led with his head, not his heart.

He had watched his mother lead with her heart, had watched her lose her life because of it. And he had lost her. He would not allow something to hold such sway over him that he would act so recklessly—not when other people needed him. As he and Hassan had needed her.

His chest ached. He ignored it. He could not afford this weakness. Not now. Not ever.

CHAPTER TWELVE

THERE were always reasons for Adham to avoid her in the weeks leading up to the wedding. He had many matters of state to handle, many press conferences and meetings with world leaders. And she was kept busy as well.

Being a sheikha was different than being a princess. In Turan she had done very little in the way of public service, but here there was an endless supply of things to do. She visited hospitals and listened to their needs, then met with the budget committee to discuss providing mobile medical units for the people who lived and worked out in the desert.

She was able to sit in on meetings with the education council and talk about the needs and concerns of the tribe she had met, was able to make it personal. She was making the most of her destiny even if her forced groom didn't seem to want to be around her.

And now the wedding was tomorrow, and the entire capital city was gearing up for a massive celebration.

They had arrived back in Maljadeed that morning. Adham had been on the phone the entire flight over, avoiding her as best he could in the luxurious cabin of the private plane.

Would he continue to be like this even after the wedding? She hoped not. They did have an heir to conceive after all. She'd found out weeks ago that neither of their times together had gotten her pregnant. But she wanted more than his child, anyway.

She ached for him, body and spirit, missed him with an intensity that took her breath away. But he was so guarded, so closed off, it seemed there was no way to reach him.

She looked down out of the window of her bedroom. Lanterns were being strung in the garden, cords woven together to create a tapestry of light over the lush landscape. It was beautiful, exotic. It was actually the wedding she would have chosen for herself.

Not simply because of the décor, because of the man. For a while she would put aside the knowledge that Adham did not love or want her and simply picture the man of her dreams standing at the head of the aisle, waiting for her, waiting for them to be joined as man and wife. For now reality could take care of itself, and she would hold onto that one image.

There was a sharp knock on the door of her room and she turned quickly. "Come in."

Her heart descended into her stomach when Adham walked through the door. She had seen him so rarely that the sight of him now sent her pulse racing. Although she knew that even if she had spent all of her time in the past two months with him she would still feel that way each time she saw him. She would never grow tired of him. Of that perfect scarred face that spoke of his bravery, his honor.

In that moment she loved him so much her whole being ached with it.

"I wasn't expecting to see you until tomorrow," she said, feeling her throat tighten, her breasts grow heavy with need.

"I have something for you." He lifted his hand and revealed a small blue box with a round brass pull on top. It reminded her of the door in Paris—the one she'd taken the picture of. She frowned and lifted the lid, her mouth dropping open when she saw the ring that was nestled in ivory silk.

She pulled the ring out and held it up, letting the late afternoon sun play across the jewels. "This is perfect," she breathed.

Tears stung her eyes as she examined the exquisitely designed piece. The lattice pattern of the platinum mirrored the Eiffel Tower, while the blue gems that were set next to the pear-shaped diamond were the same shade as the box, and her door. It was more than a ring. It was a small piece of her time with Adham. A bit of their history. This really was for her, really from him.

She held it out to him, her hand unsteady.

"Try it on," he said, his voice hard. "See if it fits as it should."

She frowned. She had expected him to put it on for her. She hadn't thought he would get on his knees—not a man like Adham, not for a marriage like theirs—but she had thought he would at least slide it onto her finger for her.

But he didn't. He only stood there, looking at her with no emotion evident in his dark eyes.

She put it on quickly, relieved when it went on easily. "Perfect," she said again, her smile forced now.

"There is a wedding band that had been made to go with it, but you will get that tomorrow."

She nodded, biting her lower lip. "Yes, okay."

It was his turn to frown. "I still haven't made you happy."

She tried harder to force the smile. "You have. I love it."

"You're crying."

She touched her cheek and her hand came away wet. "I…" There was nothing she could say. Not without sounding like a contrary female. And, truthfully, she *felt* like a contrary female. She had made such an issue over the ring, but now the ring wasn't enough. What she wanted was his love, and she didn't have it.

For one moment, seeing the ring, seeing everything that had gone into it, she had hoped. But then she'd seen his face, and her hope had dried up like water in the desert.

"Because it's so beautiful," she said, lying. He had his protection in place. She needed some too.

"I'm glad you're happy."

"Are you?"

"I am pleased that we are doing such a positive thing for our countries."

As romantic words went, they wouldn't win any awards.

I love you.

She wanted to say it. Wanted so badly to tell him how much he meant to her. But she couldn't. She had already said it once. Already faced his absolute indifference to it. He hadn't been angry, hadn't responded in kind, he had simply ignored her declaration. She couldn't face that again.

"I'll see you tomorrow," she said softly, needing him to go now. She couldn't be with him and not want to be in his arms. She couldn't stay with him like this and not tell him how much he meant to her. How she loved him more than anything.

He nodded. "Tomorrow."

She almost said it again. And if he hadn't looked like a man who was headed toward his execution she would have. Instead she waited until the door closed behind him and more tears spilled down her cheeks.

"I love you."

The last of the wedding guests were spilling out into the streets, the celebration continuing even as the palace staff began to clean up after the reception dinner.

The country was happy with its new High Sheikh, and just as happy with his new Sheikha.

Isabella's family had come. It had been wonderful to see Maximo and Alison, and their beautiful daughter. Her relationship with her brother and his wife was always easy. It had been her parents she'd been dreading. But they had been pleasant—happy, even. Likely because the deal was sealed, the contract fulfilled. Not even *she* could mess it up now.

Of course she wouldn't leave. She loved her new country, her new people. Her new husband. Her heart was here, as well as her duty.

Adham had been so handsome, the best looking groom she'd ever seen, in his loose white tunic and linen pants—a compromise between Eastern and Western fashion, as had been her cream wedding gown, with its intricate copper beading and loose, draping fabric that complemented her curves without clinging too much to them.

She had been involved in the design of her dress, which she had appreciated. She wondered if Adham had seen to that.

She closed her eyes, remembering the moment when she had walked down the aisle, when she had seen him and he had seen her for the first time. She had seen it again. That heat, the desire that had been absent from his eyes lately. He had not been able to hide it from her, not then. And when he had taken her hand in his their eyes had met, and she'd been shocked that neither of them were singed by the crack of electricity that had raced through them.

She had been filled with certainty in that moment. Now…now it had faded.

Now that she was in her room again, waiting for her husband. Waiting for her wedding night. She wasn't even certain he would come. He had been stoic at the wedding, and thanks to Umarahn customs, which did not call for the bride and groom to dance together, hadn't spent any time with her at the reception.

She wished not for the first time that she could simply read his mind. That she could know everything that went on behind that mask he put up, that wall he kept between himself and the world.

Maybe he was right and there was nothing but more rock beyond it. But maybe there was more. She believed it. She had to.

She sat on the bed, her wedding dress spread out around her. She hadn't changed because he'd seemed to like the gown so much, but now she was getting hot and itchy after hours wearing the intricate creation.

Another hour went by before she realized Adham wasn't coming to her.

She wanted to curl up and sob her heart out, to release all of her tears in the privacy of her room so that no one, especially not Adham, would ever know how much anguish she felt in that moment.

Life is simpler if you just ask for what you want.

He'd said that. And he was right. She could stay here and dissolve, give in to her tears, or she could go and get what she wanted. The Isabella who had run away from her brother's villa would have stayed in her room and wept. She might even have run away again.

But the woman she was now wouldn't do either of those things. And he was a part of making her who she was now, so he would just have to deal with it.

She opened the door to her room and walked down the hall, her bare feet not making any sound on the cold marble. She had done this before, snuck into his room at night, and then he had taken her body but ignored her love. He wouldn't ignore it tonight. She wouldn't let him.

She opened the door without knocking. Adham was standing by the window, his chest bare, the linen pants he'd worn at the wedding slung low on his hips, revealing his perfect body, his chiseled abs, trim waist and lean hips. Her heart bumped against her chest and her body ached with desire.

She shook her head. Later. There would be time for that later.

"Hi," she said, not knowing what else to say. And as greetings went it was harmless enough.

A breeze came in through the open window, ruffling his dark hair, and her heart clenched tight. She loved him so much.

Earlier, her only thought had been protecting herself, but now she realized something, watching him, looking at the guarded expression on his handsome face. She couldn't protect herself anymore. Not if she wanted him to open up to her. She had to be willing to lay herself bare to him, to put her own heart on the line, if she wanted him to be able to do the same someday.

"Adham...I love you."

He jerked back as though she'd struck him. "Bella..."

"No. Don't. Don't tell me I don't, or that I can't, because I do."

"Bella, this isn't what I want from you."

"It doesn't matter. It's the truth. I love you. Because you are the most honorable man I have ever known. Because you taught me what was important in life. Because you took me to Printemps, and took my picture in front of the Eiffel Tower."

"You don't know me," he said roughly. "Not really."

"I do."

He turned to her, his expression fierce. He walked toward her, stopping when he was close enough for her to reach out and touch. "Do not make me into some romantic paragon. I've killed men, Isabella. It doesn't matter what the reason was. There is blood on my hands."

She reached out, took his hand in hers, ran her fingers over his palm. "I don't see it."

"I do," he ground out.

She raised his hand and pressed a kiss to it. "I know that your hands have been gentle with me."

He pulled away then, the pain in his eyes apparent for a brief moment before he brought the shutters down again. "Stop," he said, his voice strangled.

"I'm being honest with you because I think it's important. I love you, Adham."

"Then I will be honest with you," he said. "I don't want you to love me."

She hadn't expected that. Not in all of the scenarios she'd played out in her mind had she expected that.

"I don't believe that. What about this?" She held her hand out to him, showed him her precious ring, the one that had been designed and crafted with such care. "This means something. I know it does."

He shook his head, his throat moving up and down. "It is just a ring."

"Not to me. I love you. You can't kill the love that I have for you. You can't make it so I don't feel it." Strength, love, desire, pain, all rolled through her body. Her heart was pounding fast and hard. "You taught me to be strong. You taught me about the importance of duty. And, I know you didn't mean to, but you've also taught me about love, about desire. So you have to deal with who I am because you were a part of making me. And I'm not backing down. I know you hate it, Adham, but you can't control the way I feel about you."

"Go, Isabella."

"What?"

"Get out. I don't want your love. I don't want you."

Her heart squeezed tight, and her lungs felt caved in, as though she couldn't breathe. "I…"

And that was when she was sure she saw fear in Adham al bin Sudar's eyes. Her warrior husband was genuinely afraid. Of her. Of her feelings. Of what they might mean to him, do to him. She remembered what he'd said about his mother—how her love for his father had made her act recklessly, how it had stolen her from him. And she knew he saw anything that had the power to control a person as a weakness.

"You're afraid, Adham. You're afraid of what you can't control, and you know that you can't tame an emotion as strong as love. You think it makes you weak, but it doesn't. I'm stronger because I love you. I'm stronger than you are because I'm not afraid, even though it hurts."

She inclined her head and turned, walking away from him, her heart feeling as though it was slowly cracking, breaking into thousands of tiny pieces.

"Where are you going?" he asked, when she reached the door.

"If you don't want me here, Adham, I won't stay." And she closed the door behind her and went back to her own room.

Adham's feet pounded on the desert sand. The night air was cold and dry in his lungs as he tried to force himself into a state of exhaustion that was strong enough to erase the last few moments of his life.

She had said he could not stop her from loving him, but he was certain that he had. The look in her eyes before she'd turned away from him had been so bleak, so desolate, he had felt the pain—her pain—reach into him and grab his heart from his chest.

She had taken it with her. But then, he suspected that Isabella had had his heart long before tonight.

And he had hurt her. He had told her the ring meant nothing. The ring...it was everything. The act of creating the design, of working with the jeweler to come up with the perfect thing for her... He had wanted so badly to remain distant from it, but it had been impossible. So he had poured everything into that design, had hoped it would get those memories, those feelings, out of him.

If anything, they had grown stronger.

He stopped and leaned forward, gripping his shins, trying to catch his breath. He didn't know how far he'd run, only that he had been desperate to drive every rational thought from his mind. It was impossible, though. No matter how hard he tried, he could only see Isabella.

She was in him. A part of him. What he felt for her was more powerful than anything he could ever remember feeling in his life. And she was right. It did terrify him. To his core.

He had faced down men holding guns, had been forced to make split-second decisions to save his life, had endured torture, and this was more frightening than any of that. To let someone mean so much to him...

Losing his parents—his mother, especially—had been so altering, so destructive to him. If not for Hassan, if not for the fact that he'd been able to pour all of his anger into protecting his brother, his country, he did not know that he would have survived it.

What would happen if he lost Isabella? Did he even know how to give her love? He had spent so many years traveling, working, burying himself in his sense of duty and honor so he didn't have to deal with real relationships. He didn't know if he would have any idea of how to open himself up now—not when he'd spent so long shutting himself down.

And she didn't deserve that. She deserved better than him. She deserved a man who had never been forced to choose between his life and the life of another man. She deserved someone who had not been so scarred by tragedy, both inside and out. Life hadn't touched her. She was beautiful. Pure and perfect. And being with him... he was afraid he might damage her in some way.

He heard the pounding of rotor blades as a helicopter flew overhead, away from the palace toward the city.

Bella.

What if she had gone? He had told her to go. He had not meant for her to leave, but he had said it. And he had hurt her. But if she left...if she left him...

He let out a fierce growl of desperation and turned back to the palace, running as though the very devil was at his heels, her name pounding in his mind in time with his footfalls.

He could not lose her. He needed her.

His heart thundered in his chest as he ran, each beat putting a crack in the protective stone until it fell away completely, leaving him raw and exposed, vulnerable. And he could feel. He could feel everything. There was no protection, no numbness, no buffer against himself and his emotions.

The pain was intense, the feeling of loss so overwhelming it stole his already shortened breath. And with that there was something else—an emotion that made him feel as though his heart might burst straight from his chest because he didn't think it could be contained inside him. It was too big, too much.

When he reached the wall of the palace he pressed in the key code and went in through the back door, hurrying quickly inside and moving around through the garden so that he could access one of the entrances near the bedchambers.

He slipped inside into Isabella's room. It was empty. The bed pristine, untouched. He saw a small dark shape on the center of the bed and he bent down to look at it. It was the ring box. And in it was the ring, along with the wedding band.

Despair gripped him. He had driven her away. He had finally done it. All of the times he had tried to rid himself of her, if not physically then emotionally, and now that he knew he needed her he had finally succeeded.

He needed her. His lovely Bella. His wife. She had shown him so many things, had taught him to see the world with new eyes. With her, things were beautiful again, fresh. He saw hope, goodness, where before he had seen nothing but the evil of the world.

She had said he had helped her become the person she was, that he had helped her grow up. But she had fixed him. Had helped him find redemption. Had pulled him from the mire he had been stuck in, from that dark hopelessness he had grown so accustomed to. He had not even realized how much he needed to be saved.

And still, in the end, he had lost her.

He picked up the box and walked outside, into the gardens. The sun was rising now; golden light shining over the palace walls, mist rising off the small pond that helped provide a cool respite from the midday heat.

He walked along the edge of it, aimless, directionless for the first time in his memory. The pain in his chest was blinding, agonizing. But he felt it.

Then he saw her. Sitting there in the midst of the garden on one of the benches, her hands folded in her lap, her cheeks wet with tears, her shoulders shaking as she sobbed.

The rose-gold light was shining on her, creating a halo around her dark hair, casting an angelic glow on her beautiful face. His wife. His love.

He loved her.

The realization staggered him. Was enough to bring him to his knees.

He walked toward her, and then he did go down on his knees, placing the ring box on the stone bench, taking her small, soft hands in his rough, scarred ones.

"Bella," he said, feeling his throat tighten, "I thought you'd left me."

She bit her lip to hold back a sob and shook her head. "No. I told you I wouldn't."

"But I said… I should not have said I didn't want you, Bella. It was a lie." He brought her hands up to his lips, pressed them against his mouth before speaking again. "And you were right. I was afraid. I was afraid of what loving you would do to me. I was afraid of what touching you would do to me. I thought it was a weakness in me that made me unable to control myself with you. But you are right. Love is not weak. Love is strong. My mother was brave. She did what she felt she had to do. I didn't see it before. I didn't understand. I do now. What she felt was beyond rational thought, beyond duty. Love is above any of those things. You helped me see that. Your strength humbles me, Bella. You're stronger than I am."

She let out a watery laugh. "No, I'm not. I'm a mess."

"Your strength inspires me," he said, raising his hand so that he could cup her cheek. "I feel as though I'm alive again for the first time since my parents died. I hadn't realized how much of myself I let die with them. Now it's like…like seeing in color when I had no clue I'd only been seeing in black and white. I love you, Sheikha Isabella Rossi al bin Sudar."

She laughed, and a tear spilled down her cheek. "That's a mouthful."

"Yes, it is, but I love saying it."

"I love *you*, Adham. I love you so much. I'm so glad I didn't check the peephole when you knocked on my hotel room door."

A hoarse chuckle escaped his lips. "I am too." He leaned in and pressed a kiss to her lips, and when he pulled away she reached forward and brushed her fingers over his cheek, wiping away moisture he hadn't realized was there.

"I love you," he whispered again. Now that he could say it, now that he knew it was true, he would never stop telling her. "I want you to know that if there was no marriage contract you would still be the woman I chose. I am not whole without you. You are my other half. I realize now that I could never have let you marry another man."

Her eyes widened. "Not even if it violated your duty?"

"Not even if it did. There is nothing greater than my love for you."

⬥ Harlequin *Presents*

Coming Next Month

from **Harlequin Presents®**. Available May 31, 2011.

#2993 FOR DUTY'S SAKE
Lucy Monroe

#2994 TAMING THE LAST ST. CLAIRE
Carole Mortimer
The Scandalous St. Claires

#2995 THE FORBIDDEN WIFE
Sharon Kendrick
The Powerful and the Pure

#2996 ONE LAST NIGHT
Melanie Milburne
The Sabbatini Brothers

#2997 THE SECRET SHE CAN'T HIDE
India Grey

#2998 THE HEIR FROM NOWHERE
Trish Morey

Coming Next Month

from **Harlequin Presents® EXTRA**. Available June 14, 2011.

#153 THE MAN WHO COULD NEVER LOVE
Kate Hewitt
Royal Secrets

#154 BEHIND THE PALACE WALLS
Lynn Raye Harris
Royal Secrets

#155 WITH THIS FLING...
Kelly Hunter
P.S. I'm Pregnant!

#156 DO NOT DISTURB
Anna Cleary
P.S. I'm Pregnant!

Visit www.HarlequinInsideRomance.com
for more information on upcoming titles!

HPECNM0511

REQUEST YOUR FREE BOOKS!

2 FREE NOVELS PLUS
2 FREE GIFTS!

PASSION GUARANTEED SEDUCTION

YES! Please send me 2 FREE Harlequin Presents® novels and my 2 FREE gifts (gifts are worth about $10). After receiving them, if I don't wish to receive any more books, I can return the shipping statement marked "cancel." If I don't cancel, I will receive 6 brand-new novels every month and be billed just $4.05 per book in the U.S. or $4.74 per book in Canada. That's a saving of at least 15% off the cover price! It's quite a bargain! Shipping and handling is just 50¢ per book in the U.S. and 75¢ per book in Canada.* I understand that accepting the 2 free books and gifts places me under no obligation to buy anything. I can always return a shipment and cancel at any time. Even if I never buy another book, the two free books and gifts are mine to keep forever.

106/306 HDN FC55

Name _____ (PLEASE PRINT) _____

Address _____ Apt. #

City _____ State/Prov. _____ Zip/Postal Code

Signature (If under 18, a parent or guardian must sign)

Mail to the **Reader Service:**
IN U.S.A.: P.O. Box 1867, Buffalo, NY 14240-1867
IN CANADA: P.O. Box 609, Fort Erie, Ontario L2A 5X3

Not valid for current subscribers to Harlequin Presents books.

**Are you a current subscriber to Harlequin Presents books
and want to receive the larger-print edition?
Call 1-800-873-8635 or visit www.ReaderService.com.**

* Terms and prices subject to change without notice. Prices do not include applicable taxes. Sales tax applicable in N.Y. Canadian residents will be charged applicable taxes. Offer not valid in Quebec. This offer is limited to one order per household. All orders subject to credit approval. Credit or debit balances in a customer's account(s) may be offset by any other outstanding balance owed by or to the customer. Please allow 4 to 6 weeks for delivery. Offer available while quantities last.

Your Privacy—The Reader Service is committed to protecting your privacy. Our Privacy Policy is available online at www.ReaderService.com or upon request from the Reader Service.

We make a portion of our mailing list available to reputable third parties that offer products we believe may interest you. If you prefer that we not exchange your name with third parties, or if you wish to clarify or modify your communication preferences, please visit us at www.ReaderService.com/consumerschoice or write to us at Reader Service Preference Service, P.O. Box 9062, Buffalo, NY 14269. Include your complete name and address.

HP11

Harlequin® Blaze™ brings you
New York Times *and* USA TODAY *bestselling author*
Vicki Lewis Thompson with three new steamy titles
from the bestselling miniseries SONS OF CHANCE

Chance isn't just the last name of these rugged
Wyoming cowboys—it's their motto, too!

Read on for a sneak peek at the first title,
SHOULD'VE BEEN A COWBOY

Available June 2011 only from Harlequin® Blaze™.

"Thanks for not turning on the lights," Tyler said. "I'm a mess."

"Not in my book." Even in low light, Alex had a good view of her yellow shirt plastered to her body. It was all he could do not to reach for her, mud and all. But the next move needed to be hers, not his.

She slicked her wet hair back and squeezed some water out of the ends as she glanced upward. "I like the sound of the rain on a tin roof."

"Me, too."

She met his gaze briefly and looked away. "Where's the sink?"

"At the far end, beyond the last stall."

Tyler's running shoes squished as she walked down the aisle between the rows of stalls. She glanced sideways at Alex. "So how much of a cowboy are you these days? Do you ride the range and stuff?"

"I ride." He liked being able to say that. "Why?"

"Just wondered. Last summer, you were still a city boy. You even told me you weren't the cowboy type, but you're...different now."

He wasn't sure if that was a good thing or a bad thing. Maybe she preferred city boys to cowboys. "How am I different?"

"Well, you dress differently, and your hair's a little longer. Your face seems a little more chiseled, but maybe that's because of your hair. Also, there's something else, something harder to define, an attitude…"

"Are you saying I have an attitude?"

"Not in a bad way. It's more like a quiet confidence."

He was flattered, but still he had to laugh. "I just admitted a while ago that I have all kinds of doubts about this event tomorrow. That doesn't seem like quiet confidence to me."

"This isn't about your job, it's about…your…" She took a deep breath. "It's about your sex appeal, okay? I have no business talking about it, because it will only make me want to do things I shouldn't do." She started toward the end of the barn. "Now, where's that sink? We need to get cleaned up and go back to the house. Dinner is probably ready, and I—"

He spun her around and pulled her into his arms, mud and all. "Let's do those things." Then he kissed her, knowing that she would kiss him back, knowing that this time he would take that kiss where he wanted it to go. And she would let him.

Follow Tyler and Alex's wild adventures in
SHOULD'VE BEEN A COWBOY
Available June 2011 only from Harlequin® Blaze™
wherever books are sold.

Copyright © 2011 by Vicki Lewis Thompson

Harlequin *Presents*®

brings you

USA TODAY *bestselling author*

Lucy Monroe

*with her new installment
in the much-loved miniseries*

Royal Brides

Proud, passionate rulers—
marriage is by royal decree!

Meet Zahir and Asad—two powerful, brooding sheikhs
and masters of all they survey. They need brides,
and marriage in their kingdoms is by royal decree!

Capture a slice of royal life in this enthralling sheikh saga!

Coming in June 2011:
FOR DUTY'S SAKE

**Available wherever
Harlequin Presents® books are sold.**

www.eHarlequin.com

HP12993